CW00767622

This book is to be retu

50389

IT ISN'T OVER UNTIL THE FAT LADY SINGS

JFS LIBRARY

IT ISN'T OVER UNTIL
THE FAT LADY SINGS

All the love, passion, jealousy and murder that is so gloriously sung about in some of the world's greatest operas has been the inspiration for the stories in this collection. Some retain the mythical quality of the original stories, others unashamedly leap into the twentieth century or are a tantalizing mixture of both. The names of the operas which inspired these short stories are given at the beginning of each.

IT ISN'T OVER UNTIL
THE FAT LADY SINGS

Edited by
MICK GOWAR

THE BODLEY HEAD
London

50389

J. F. S. LIBRARY

175 Camden Road **NW1 9HD**

This collection copyright © 1992 Mick Gowar
Each story is copyright © 1992 by its named author

First published in Great Britain 1992 by
The Bodley Head Children's Book
an imprint of Random House UK Limited
20 Vauxhall Bridge Road, London SW1V 2SA

Random House Australia (Pty) Limited
20 Alfred Street, Sydney, NSW 2061, Australia

Random House New Zealand Limited
18 Poland Road, Glenfield, Auckland 10, New Zealand

Random House South Africa (Pty) Limited
PO Box 337, Bergvlei 2012, South Africa

A CIP catalogue record for this book is
available from the British Library

ISBN 0–370–31695–9

Phototypeset in Bembo by Intype, London
Printed and bound in Great Britain by
Cox & Wyman Ltd, Reading

CONTENTS

MADAM BUTTERFLY

Jan Mark

Based on the opera
MADAMA BUTTERFLY
Composer: Giacomo Puccini (1858–1924)
Librettists: Luigi Illica and Giuseppe Giacosa,
after David Belasco
First performed: Milan 1904

Ford was missing his wife. Louisa remained in New York, not merely on the far side of the Pacific Ocean, but on the far side of the continent that lay beyond it. Twirling the globe in his office he tried to calculate the shortest journey that separated them, across Asia and the Atlantic . . . over the North Pole . . . if only a man could fly. Ford put aside his calculations and confided in a colleague who had been longer in Nagasaki and understood how things could be arranged.

Ford and his colleagues were engineers, imparting American skills to their Japanese hosts, but ahead of the civilians had come the Navy, spearheaded by Commodore Perry, in '53. The Navy had, with its customary dispatch, discovered an ideal system for easing a man's solitude, one which provided the consolations of married life with the comforts of home; and all for a ridiculously low outlay.

It appeared to Ford that a wife could be hired more or less by the month, along with a house. Plenty of Japanese girls made a living that way. This was not, after all, the United States of America, where a woman these days might go for a school-teacher, or even a doctor, were she so inclined.

'And when you've had enough,' explained Ford's knowledgeable friend, 'just pay the lady off and return to your wife.'

'What about the lady?' Ford asked, not at all sure that such a delightful arrangement could really be so simple.

'Why, she waits a decent interval – maybe a day – and sets up with her next husband. They aren't like us, you know,' said the friend. 'Japanese girls ain't brought up to think for themselves. You may buy 'em and sell 'em. If Papa takes it into his head to marry them to a Barbarian – that's us, you know – then off they go and do it.'

'But don't they mind?'

'Oh, I dare say they may *mind*, but it don't signify. If your mousme cuts up when you leave, you can toss a few more yen her way and tell her you'll be back when the robins nest.'

There was some uneasy laughter around the room at this, and Ford left under the impression that one or two of the fellows disapproved of the practice of 'marrying' a mousme. There were Barbarians, foreigners, who had contracted genuine marriages with well-connected Japanese women, but the young girls, the mousmes, wedded by the month, were not well-connected or, if they ever had been, had since fallen upon hard times.

Ford saw nothing distressing in the idea of girls being sold, or selling themselves; it was, after all, the oldest profession open to them, as that fellow Kipling had written; not pure girls, like his Louisa but, well, *other* sorts of girls. Nevertheless, that half-articulated protest that followed the sally about robins nesting . . . was it perhaps a vulgar Japanese joke?

The friend had offered to introduce him to a marriage broker, who would undertake to find a suitable bride, but before Ford could act upon this offer he found himself obliged to call in at the American Consulate to send a telegram. He had met the Consul, one Sharpless, on a couple of social occasions, but there was something about the man's manner that depressed him. 'Too long in the Orient,' Ford thought, whenever he saw the sun-yellowed complexion of the Consul, the lugubrious moustache and drooping eyelids. A fellow might almost suppose that he had a guilty secret although, as Ford was beginning to discover, there seemed to be precious little out here for a man to feel guilty about.

Still, even if not too long in the Orient, Sharpless had certainly been there long enough to know his way about. After he had dictated the cable, Ford said, casually as he thought, 'By the way, Sharpless, is there anything in this business about robins nesting?'

Upon the Consul's withered cheek appeared a discoloration that might have been taken for a blush; and in his eye a look that threatened anger.

'May I inquire, sir,' he said, 'who put you up to asking me that?'

'Why – no one. That is, no one put me up to it,' Ford stammered. 'But I heard it said—'

'It was a cruel joke, uttered by a thoughtless man to a girl who believed that her husband would tell her the truth,' Sharpless said, 'and I, God forgive me, was too craven to disabuse her. Now, if you have no further business here—'

'A girl?' Ford said, discomfited. 'A mousme?'

'The word is *museme*,' said the Consul. 'It is Japanese for daughter or a young girl. A man who lies to a young girl is no man at all, to my mind, and Cho-Cho-San was very young. She ought to have been at school or playing with her dolls. But that heartless fool made *her* into a doll, and played with her. Still, I dare say you know all this, or you would not have troubled to stop by and taunt me with your talk of nesting robins.'

'I assure you, sir, I knew nothing,' Ford said. 'The subject came up as a consequence—'

'As a consequence of your deciding to take a wife?' the Consul interjected. 'One hears these things. I understood that you were already married.'

'This is simply an arrangement,' Ford said. 'You know how things are.'

'Yes, I do,' Sharpless replied. 'May I ask whom you intend to "marry"?'

'Well, some geisha, I suppose. A girl of that sort.'

'Of what sort?' Sharpless said. 'A geisha is not a prostitute – oh, don't begin to protest. True, some of them consent to become a "second wife" and understand what they are about, but their calling is to create a congenial and civilized atmosphere in the tea houses. Their training takes years. Make sure your second wife understands what she is about, sir. Be square with her.'

'What do you take me for?' Ford asked, heatedly.

'I take you for what I see; another heartless young fool who intends to borrow a girl as thoughtlessly as he might borrow his sister's doll. I see,' Sharpless said, 'what I have seen before.'

'What did you see – before?' Ford said, perceiving that the Consul was in deadly earnest.

Sharpless took a chair and waved Ford into another, on the far side of the desk.

'I saw a young naval lieutenant named Benjamin Franklin Pinkerton – fine upstanding names, don't you think – who decided to set himself up with a wife while his ship was in port. He was already engaged, mind you, to an American girl – he hadn't gone quite so far down that road as you – but he went to a *nakoda* – I see you already know what a *nakoda* does – a man called Goro; oh, it's the same one, is it? Well, Goro found him a bride, the girl I told you about, Cho-Cho-San. She'd come rather late to being a geisha; she was about fifteen, and hardly more than an apprentice. Usually they begin to train very young; at six years, six months and six days, to be exact. Her family had come down in the world, in fact her father had been obliged to commit suicide as a matter of honour, and she'd had to earn her own living. Pinkerton rented a house that Goro found for him, up on Higachi Hill, and Cho-Cho-San came with it. He told her he'd rented it for nine hundred and ninety-nine years – which was true, in a way. As a foreigner he had no option. What he didn't bother to explain to her was that the tenancy lapsed if he failed to pay the rent. That fell due every month. Nine hundred and ninety-nine years,' Sharpless said. 'It must have seemed like eternity to her.

'It was a regular Japanese house, mainly made out of *shoji* – those paper screens you see every-where, in a flower garden overlooking the harbour. The climb to that hill-top is crippling, but it was what he wanted. A secluded haven of blossoms to come home to and a good little wife waiting for him. That was what he got, and all for a hundred yen. She thought it was a fortune – promised to be a careful housekeeper so as not to cost him any more money.'

'She spoke English, then?' Ford said.

'Very well; but not well enough for a wife. Most women can tell when their husbands are

8

lying, but she wasn't *that* well up in our language. Took everything he said for Gospel truth, even after—

'Well, I went to the wedding. It was hideous, embarrassing; twittering girlfriends, gushing aunties, drunken uncle, badly behaved nephew.'

'Sounds like a regular wedding party,' Ford remarked, with feeling.

'Except in one respect. In the usual way of things you'd know that these people were going to become your relatives and do your best to get along with them. After all, you'd be seeing them often enough. But Pinkerton – he'd already insulted the servants – didn't try any such thing. He baited the uncle, tried to get his mother-in-law tipsy—'

'Didn't she mind?'

'The mother-in-law?'

'The girl. The bride.'

'I don't think she fairly took in what he was doing. She was already besotted. She was showing off the house to her friends, boasting a little. He'd had locks fitted to everything; they thought that was incredible. It was,' Sharpless said. 'Paper screens with locks on. He said it was to keep out those who were out, and in, those who were in. She was a little taken aback,' he went on, 'when she realized that the people he intended to keep out were her own family, but she hardly protested. Her was her husband. He could do no wrong.

She'd as good as admitted that at first she didn't much care for the idea of marrying a Barbarian, but she changed her mind after she'd seen him.

'I guess none of this would have mattered if only she hadn't taken it all so seriously. She'd left everything behind except a few little trinkets, a pipe, some silk handkerchiefs. Tiny things, she kept them in the sleeves of her kimono. But as well, she had some *Otoke*, little statuettes that represented the souls of her ancestors, very precious to her. But she threw them away, actually *threw* them, to prove her devotion to her American husband. What is more, she had been to the Mission here, to see the priest. She was willing to give up everything for her husband, even her religion.

'One thing she kept, though, in spite of his teasing; that was the ceremonial sword that the Mikado had sent to her father; a delicate hint that he should commit suicide. The characters on the blade read, "Better to die with honour, when one can no longer live with honour".

'I stayed to witness the marriage and, incidentally, to witness Pinkerton toasting his future American wife at the same time as he toasted his Japanese bride. The girlfriends were all congratulating her as Madam Butterfly – that was the name she used at work, in the tea house, but she wouldn't have it. "Not Madam Butterfly," she told them. "Mrs Pinkerton." That should have warned us.

'Well, I left after the formalities so I missed

the worst part. I got that later, from Pinkerton. The party was going badly down-hill; Uncle Yamikade in his cups, singing inappropriate songs, the child stuffing himself fit to be sick, the girl-friends making jealous remarks, when the *other* uncle burst in. He was a priest himself, a *Bonze*, and he'd heard about the visits to the Mission. He cursed them. First he cursed Pinkerton, who couldn't have cared less, then he cursed Cho-Cho-San, ranting and shouting. Pinkerton lost his temper, told him to hold his jaw and get out; and he got out, taking all the guests with him, girlfriends and aunties, uncles and Mama. I believe that was the last time she saw any of them.

'I don't know if she realized what she had committed herself to, but she might as well have landed herself alone in a foreign country, this little American outpost with everything Japanese locked out. There were servants, of course; a cook, a houseboy and the maid, Miss Suzuki, but the family and friends were gone – banished. Banished by Pinkerton and the *Bonze*.

'I doubt if she cared, at first, she was so in love with him. What newly-weds ever thought of what would happen next week, or next year? Tomorrow is a million days away. Perhaps, some-times, if she had a moment alone, she might have asked herself what she had lost, but what could she know of what might have been? Fifteen. She was fifteen,' the Consul said.

'I suppose he loved her too, as far as he was

able to love. He talked of her to his mess-mates –
and to me, but he might as well have been boasting
of a piece of fine porcelain that he had bought
cheap; his Japanese doll. The trouble was, she no
longer perceived of herself as Japanese. To her
mind, she was the American wife of an American
citizen. When she spoke of "her country" she
meant the United States, not Japan. I saw her a
few times, at the house, but he didn't take her
about. He was proud of his bargain, but mainly as
regards his cleverness in acquiring it. She used to
ask me about America – and American laws; very
interested in how American women lived. You
could see which way her thoughts were going: Mrs
B F Pinkerton, walking down Fifth Avenue on her
husband's arm. She must have wondered sometimes when she would meet his friends, his family;
how she would enter American society, but she
was too well-trained to ask questions. And she was
happy.

    'Someone had told her what Americans do to
butterflies – catching them in a net and impaling
them on pins. She could not see that this was
exactly what had happened to her.'

    'Shame.' Ford stared across the desk at the
Consul, mildly moved by the story of little Madam
Butterfly and her ill-conceived hopes of American
Citizenship, but then he remembered how the con-
versation had started. This rather common-place
tale of a red-blooded man and a credulous girl was

hardly the stuff of tragedy. Was there more? He waited.

Sharpless resumed. 'After about three months the *Abraham Lincoln* – that was his ship – was ordered out of port. He had to go – she understood that. She'd made it her business to become a model American naval officer's wife; not to weep or cling when her man sailed away, although I guess she wept when he'd gone. Don't imagine that she was on the quayside to see him off, oh no. *I* know where she was,' Sharpless said. 'That house overlooks the harbour. He'd bought a telescope and set it up in the garden to watch for signals from the ship, and he'd left it with her. That day she would have stood in her garden with the telescope, watching the *Abraham Lincoln* sail away, trying to find her husband among the figures on deck. He told her he'd be back when the robins nested.'

'Ah.' Ford recognized the unfortunate words. 'What did he mean?'

'What do you think he meant? He had no intention of returning – no idea if he ever could. He had no more notion than any other sailor of where his calling would take him next. I'm inclined to allow, when in a forgiving mood, that he'd never meant to let her think he would be faithful, that when the time came to part he'd pay her off and say goodbye for ever, but when the time did come and he saw how she had deceived herself, and how he had let her, he had not the courage to be honest. He said he would come back and she believed him. I suppose that when you left Mrs Ford you told her you would return?'

'Do you suggest that I would lie to my wife?'

'And she believed you?'

'Of course she did. She knows I will.'

'Madam Butterfly saw not one jot of difference between Mrs Ford and Mrs Pinkerton. You think she was presumptuous?'

'Well, I say, it's hardly the same thing, is it?' Ford protested. 'An American woman and a Japanese girl.'

'So, there she was,' Sharpless said, 'alone on her hill-top with Suzuki – that was the maid, though by-and-by, I guess, she became more than a maid. Cho-Cho-San received no social calls, American or Japanese. The family had disowned her, the Americans scarcely knew she existed. Two young women together . . . if they were not enemies, they must become friends. And Cho-Cho-San needed a friend.

'Suzuki said that not a day went by but that she ran a dozen times to her telescope, watching the harbour, frantic with excitement whenever she saw a ship hull-down on the horizon, but never despairing, for she never doubted. One fine day he would come back. She had only to wait.

'But they had also to live. Pinkerton had left her some money. He really imagined that she would go back to her old work in the tea house when he left, if she did not straightaway find another protector; the money was no more than a parting gift. But she thought it was her housekeeping, to last until he returned. God knows how they survived. She dismissed the servants, though Suzuki stayed, unpaid, and somehow they scraped along. Goro tried to help. He's not a bad fellow and he did his best. It wasn't as though Cho-Cho was shunned by all. She was famously beautiful and accomplished, more than one man wanted to marry her and Goro tried to persuade her, but she would not listen. She was already a married woman, was she not? An abandoned wife, living near starvation, but still a wife, whose husband would come back. Do not think of mousmes and geishas, boy; think of Mrs Ford who waits for *you*. That is how it was for her. She said he would return. And she was right.

'It was about three years since he left when we received word that the *Abraham Lincoln* was due back at Nagasaki. I had a letter from Pinkerton. I'd forgotten about him – and her, to tell you the truth, for I hadn't seen her since he left. The letter was affable, that was his way. He wrote to ask after Cho-Cho-San, asked me to go and see her. "Perhaps she has forgotten me," he wrote. Maybe he believed that. What he meant was that he *hoped* she had forgotten him. He was married now. His wife was with him. I took it that Mrs Pinkerton knew nothing of her husband's earlier arrangement and he was afraid of a scene. You can imagine how I felt. If I'd thought of her at all, I suppose, I'd assumed that she was back in the tea house, and doing rather well moreover, because Pinkerton had made me responsible for keeping up the rent. But that letter made me afraid. Because *he* was afraid.

'I went straightaway, before she heard from some other quarter, and on the way up the hill I overtook Goro. Poor Goro. There he was, with word of another suitor eager for the hand of Madam Butterfly, Prince Yamadori. A wonderful chance for her, but Goro was afraid she might refuse him as she had refused the others. I dare say he would have brought me up to date with news of the household but before we got there, as we were going through the garden we could hear Cho-Cho-San and Suzuki, arguing. Suzuki was a sceptical girl. She'd got the measure of Pinkerton right away, but I guess she'd kept quiet. Now Cho-Cho-San was shouting at her, insisting that one day they would see his ship in the harbour and he would come back, up the hill, to claim her. She had it all planned, how she would hide at first, and then spring out to surprise him; the way children do. But there was nothing childish in that voice; I heard the hysteria of a desperate woman.

'She recognized me – after so long! But I would never have recognized her. She had aged – more than three years. Grief and hardship had changed her lovely face, but the worst thing was her gown. She no longer wore the kimono, instead she had on an ugly mockery of what she imagined an American woman might wear, I suppose she and Suzuki had made it. Her hair was screwed into a knot – she looked like a scrub-woman. But she received us graciously. She received *me* graciously. Goro, I felt, was something of a gadfly. She offered me American cigarettes, made small talk. There was a picture of President Roosevelt on the wall, alongside one of Pinkerton. Two heroes.

'I tried to find the courage to deliver my message, I swear it, Ford. I meant to be straight with her, but I told her right away that I had a letter from Pinkerton, and she was off, trying to be calm, but talking, talking, all about when did those damned robins nest in America, maybe not so often as here in Japan. Then Goro shoved his oar in and suddenly Prince Yamadori was announced. He hadn't known I'd be there, of course, but he carried it off very well, delivering his speech about dying of love for Butterfly, but she wasn't having it. She insisted that she was already married (and now she knew about Pinkerton's letter, though she didn't know what was in it), reminding Yamadori that he too was already married and divorced, several times over. She read him a lecture on our American divorce law – or her notion of it – and then threw him out, more or less; in the nicest possible way, of course. I felt keenly for Yamadori. He could see what lay ahead for her . . . but in the end he went, with Goro.

'I tried again to read the letter but now she

was so excited she didn't take in a word of it and I couldn't bring myself to read it all. I asked her instead what she would do if Pinkerton did not return. She said she would go back to the tea house, which was what I'd assumed she had already done. Or else, she said, better to die. Then I begged her over and over again to reconsider Yamadori's offer, but it was no good. She was enraged. All her training deserted her, she almost ordered me out of the house, but when I apologized she was all gentleness again, and at her most gentle, she struck her hardest blow.

' "Even if he has forgotten me," she cried, "could he forget this?" She ran out of the room and returned with a child in her arms.

'Her child; hers and Pinkerton's.

'I hadn't known there was a child.

'And such a child, fair-haired, blue-eyed, but with his mother's fineness. Pinkerton's a big fellow. She was chattering to him, as mothers will to children. "Did you hear the gentleman?" she said. "He thinks I should go back to dancing for a living. Well, if I do, I'll take you on my shoulder through the town. The Emperor himself will see you with those blue eyes and bow before you. No Japanese ever had such blue eyes," she said.

'Her American son. She'd named him Sorrow, imagining it to be the kind of joke that would appeal to Pinkerton. He loved a paradox. She thought that when Pinkerton came home, Sorrow would become Joy. She thought,' Sharpless said, 'that the name was inappropriate. That was the joke.

'I had to get away. I could not bear it. But as I went another row broke out. Suzuki had found Goro hanging about in the garden, and the two of them set on him. He'd been trying to tell Suzuki that in America a child like that would be an outcast. Cho-Cho grabbed the ceremonial sword that she kept on the shrine and Goro ran for his life. I didn't mention the shrine, did I?' Sharpless said, sadly. 'I guess our Christian God had failed to come up to the mark and she'd gone back to the old faith. Anyway, Goro passed me at high speed. I'm surprised he didn't break his neck on that steep path, and just then there was a great boom from below, in the harbour. It was the cannon, signalling that a ship was entering port. I looked back, up the hill, and there was Cho-Cho-San *flying* to the telescope, with Suzuki and the baby behind her. I heard her scream, "The Stars and Stripes! The *Abraham Lincoln*!"

'I wish I could end there,' the Consul said; 'Madam Butterfly in triumph, proved right in spite of everything the others had said. Later, Suzuki told me what happened. It was the last time she spoke to me. I've passed her once or twice in the streets. She looks, and looks away.

'They thought he would come at once and fell over themselves to prepare the house. When I saw the garden next day it was stripped, as barren as winter. They took every flower to decorate the rooms, while Sorrow danced about under their feet, waving an American flag that his mother had given him. Then Cho-Cho-San took off her American dress and put on her bridal kimono. She painted her face and Suzuki dressed her hair. Poor child, she was afraid he would no longer find her beautiful. She did not deceive herself about the loss of her looks. Poor Cho-Cho, poor little girl.

'Then they drew the *shoji* – the screens – for night was falling. Cho-Cho-San wet her finger and made three holes in the paper for them to look through, one each for herself and Suzuki and one very low down, for the baby. Then they settled to watch, sure that he would be with them in an hour. It grew dark. The moon rose. He did not come. By and by the baby fell asleep, but Cho-Cho and Suzuki remained at the *shoji*, watching. Suzuki was kneeling and at last she slept where she knelt. When she woke it was to find Cho-Cho shaking her shoulder. It was morning, and still he had not come to her.

'Suzuki knew then, but dared not say. She persuaded Cho-Cho-San to rest for a while, with the baby. That maid and I were comrades in misfortune, we sceptics, but she was braver than I. She spoke her mind. What she did not guess was that at that very moment, Pinkerton was only minutes from the door.

'I had barely arrived back at the Consulate that last evening when Pinkerton strode in, and he was not alone. A young woman was with him, a fine tall, handsome American, like himself. He greeted me like an old friend, as I suppose I was, and introduced her. "Kate, this is Sharpless, our excellent Consul. Sharpless, this is my wife." And then, while Kate was given tea, I took him aside and told him what had been happening up in that little house on Higachi Hill, told him that he was now a father. He kept his countenance well, but Kate could see at once that something was amiss. They left soon after and I guess he must have made a clean breast of it to her in his frank and manly fashion. We Americans are famously straight – with each other.

'Anyhow, next morning they were back at the Consulate. Kate had acted like a regular trump, he said, forgiven him everything and was even prepared to take the child to bring up as their own son. After all, if he was as blond and blue-eyed as I'd said, why, who'd know the truth? I tried to explain that Cho-Cho-San rather regarded the child as hers and would never consent to parting with him.

' "Oh, but she must!" cried Kate. "After all, he is an American child. We can't leave him to grow up – *here*." Everything she thought she knew about Japan was in that word. But on one point at least she and Cho-Cho-San were in agreement;

little Sorrow was an American child. They persuaded me to go up to the house with them and lay Kate's modest proposal before Cho-Cho-San. I tell you, Ford, I never before or since made a journey with greater reluctance, with a heavier heart. It was a cruel climb, up that hill, and as we ascended I saw that Pinkerton was at last beginning to understand what he had done. As we passed each familiar landmark he grew more silent, but Kate was chattering on – our Yankee colleges are producing some formidable women; I was breathless by half-way up Higachi Hill – making plans for the baby, confiding that she'd wait till she'd seen him before deciding whether or not she could pass him off as her own back in Norfolk, Virginia.

'At last the house came into sight, with the telescope on its tripod against the sky. We both, Pinkerton and I, exclaimed over the garden. As I told you, there was not a flower left in it.

'Kate had fallen quiet. Perhaps, in her quick-witted way, she had divined the reason for the position of the telescope. She said that she would wait in the garden out of sight, to begin with, so we, Pinkerton and I, went to the door without her. It was Suzuki who came out to us and – oh, such emotions crossed her face when she saw us. Incredulity, joy, relief – then doubt, suspicion.

' "We waited all night for you," she cried. "We took every flower and decked the house and then we stood at the *shoji* until you should come.

Now she is sleeping." In her eyes was the unspoken question, "Why did you not come at once?" And she looked at me. Again the unspoken question; "Why are *you* here? This is not the time for strangers." Then she looked beyond us and saw Kate.

' "Who is that lady?" she said. Her voice was shrill with fear. She knew. I swear she knew, but she would not allow herself to believe.

'Pinkerton tried to quieten her, but she could not stop.

' "Who is it? Who is it?"

' "She came with me," he said, lamely.

'I could not stand it. "She's his wife," I said.

'Suzuki cried out once and fell to the ground, as if struck down.

'I lifted her up and tried to explain how we had come early, hoping to find her alone, hoping that she would help us; help us explain to Cho-Cho-San that Kate wanted to take the child. I begged her to go and speak to Kate herself, to bring her to the house. For I doubted if any of us had the courage to tell Cho-Cho-San what her own eyes would tell her when she saw Kate.

'Meanwhile, Pinkerton had entered the house and discovered where the flowers had gone, discovered his portrait – and Teddy Roosevelt. It was all coming back to him now, how happy they had been, how he had deceived her. For I saw now how he had been deceiving himself for three years, wilfully forgetting, and he could not bear it. He had not the courage to stay and confront the first Mrs Pinkerton when she met the second, now he knew that very far from forgetting him she had counted every second until he should return.

'He pressed some money into my hand, a large sum, for *her*, and fled in tears, skulking on the footpath until we had done his miserable work for him. When Suzuki saw this, she brought Kate in from the garden.

' "Then you will tell her?" Kate was saying. "You will explain that I shall love him as my own son – persuade her that she can trust me?" Ah, we were all so brave, were we not, we three tall Americans; we could not face one little Japanese lady.

'Suzuki promised to break the news to her and asked us to leave them alone together, but it was too late. There was a call from the bedroom, Cho-Cho-San had heard voices and came running. Suzuki tried to stop her, but she rushed in.

' "He's here! Where is he? Where is he hiding?" She searched the room. It took only seconds.

'She saw me – and her face clouded. Then she saw Kate and Suzuki, weeping. I tried to approach her, but she shrank away, afraid; afraid to ask another question. But she asked it; it was the wrong question.

'She said, "He lives?"

'Would that we could have replied, "Alas, no." We might have shared that sorrow.

'Only Suzuki found the voice to answer, "Yes."

' "But he will come here no more?"

' "Never again," said Suzuki. At last it was said, the waiting was over – but there was more.

' "He is here, in Nagasaki – since yesterday?"

' "Yes," Suzuki said.

' "And who is this lady?" Cho-Cho-San asked us. Somehow she understood that this was the source of her grief.

'Kate had spent her time alone in the garden composing pretty speeches, but all she could say was, "Forgive me, it was not my fault."

'She started to approach Cho-Cho-San, but Cho-Cho motioned her away. Ah, she was proud, then; in possession, true to herself. Perhaps inside her head some voice said, "This is the real Mrs Pinkerton. I was the first." But she was no longer Mrs Pinkerton, even in her own mind. She was Madam Butterfly once more.

' "Do not touch me," she said, and there was a long silence before she continued, very calmly, "How long is it since he married you?"

' "A year," said Kate, and she might have added, "We were promised long before that," but she did not.

'Instead she cried, "Will you let me do something for the child?" and when Cho-Cho-San did not reply, thinking no doubt to repulse some offer of charity, condescendingly made, she went on, "I will love him as though he were my own. Let us have him – it will be best for him in the end."

'She heard this woman, who had taken her husband, calmly ask to take her son too, as though she, Cho-Cho-San, had only been a wet-nurse, rearing him till he was needed.

'Kate persisted. "We can give him a better life, he will be ours, our own." She imagined she was being generous.

'Cho-Cho-San did not say yes. She said only, "There is no happier lady than you under heaven. May you remain so. I would be pleased if you were to tell him that I too shall find peace."

'Kate was much moved and held out her hand, but Cho-Cho-San would not take it, though she was able to speak kindly. "No," she said, "not that. Go now."

'Kate had the delicacy to withdraw, but as she went by me, not quite grasping what had passed between them, she said, "And can he have his son?"

'Cho-Cho-San heard and answered, "I will give him his son if he comes himself to fetch him. Tell him to climb the hill one last time, in half an hour."

'Suzuki took Kate out. I was left with Cho-Cho-San – and the money Pinkerton had given me for her. I knew she would not take it, but I had to offer it. What else could I do? I did not know what to say. Such shame . . .

'*She* tried to comfort *me*. "At least despair

brings peace," she said. "Hoping and dreaming do not. Take back the money. I shall not need it."

'I should have known what she meant.

' "Shall we meet again?" I asked her.

' "Climb the hill in half an hour," she said.

'I went out of the house and down through the garden to the footpath where the Pinkertons were waiting. Kate had already passed on the message. He had taken out his watch.

'So we stood there, while in the house the little drama was played out.

'Suzuki wanted to stay with her friend, but Cho-Cho-San told her to watch the child. She was going to rest, she said. Suzuki knew what kind of a rest she spoke of and begged to stay, but she sent her away. Then she took down her father's ceremonial sword from the shrine. She kept it covered by a white veil, in piety. Remember there were words inscribed on it; "Better to die with honour, when one can no longer live with honour".

'Suzuki, at the door, saw what she was about and pushed the little boy towards his mother. For an instant she thought her ploy had succeeded. Cho-Cho-San flung down the sword and threw her arms around the child, half-smothering him with kisses. But she was resolute. She sat her little son on a stool, gave him his American flag to play with and gently bandaged his eyes as she said farewell to him. She would not have him see the manner of her going. Suzuki, knowing now that she was beyond all persuading, could only watch as she went back behind the screen and drove the blade into her throat. There was no going back now, but longing for one last look at her son, she wound the white veil about her throat and staggered toward him.

'And at that moment, Pinkerton clapped shut his watch, and like a man going into battle said, "It is time." Leaving Kate on the path we went back together to the house.

'It was silent. He called, "Butterfly?"

'No answer.

'He called again, alarmed. "Butterfly! Butterfly!"

'It was the last sound she heard, his voice calling her name.

'We rushed in. The child, in his blindfold, sat on the floor, playing with the Stars and Stripes. She lay beside him. Did she see us? She knew that we were there, knew *he* was there. She had just enough strength to point: There, sir, is your son: and died.

'Pinkerton fell to his knees beside – his wife. I took the child, and wept.'

Ford shifted uncomfortably, seeing that the Consul might weep again.

'Confounded shame,' he muttered. 'Still, they aren't all like that, are they?'

'I beg your pardon?' Sharpless said.

'Not all like Madam What's-her-name. To-To-San. I mean, most of them seem to be quite sensible.'

'Oh, quite,' Sharpless said. 'Some of them might also be said to be like us, happy to live with dishonour. But all the same, Ford, spare me the embarrassment of having to refuse you, and do not ask me to your wedding.'

THE RHINEGOLD

Bryony Lavery

Based on the opera
DER RING DES NIBELUNGEN: DAS
RHEINGOLD
Composer and librettist: Richard Wagner (1813–83)
First performed: Munich 1869

I have been feeling like shit.
My belly always seems like it's got a dead rat rolling around in it.
I jump at the slightest sound.
The palms of my hands are slick and hot with sweat.
Thirteen times now has my face broken out in an angry red sea of yellow-headed pimples, aching red spots and shoal upon shoal of blackheads.
I feel stagnant. I feel like a slimy green pond in the middle of a dark wood. I feel like stale soup.
I've tried every cure. Green vegetables. Fresh water. I've rolled naked in the snows in winter, steamed myself in sulphur baths in the summer.
Nothing's worked.
I've really been feeling like shit.

I've thought I was dying.
So I left Germany and headed for Italy.
Slow boats and trains across the map and I'm here in Spezia.
And here, in the soft warm air, I begin to realize what is wrong with me.
There is such a story stuck inside me and now, here, it's beginning to break through me.

*

Tonight I took a long walk, then I tried to sleep a little on the couch in my room. And I slipped into a trance-like state. There was a rushing and roaring in my head and my mind was filled with broken chords whose melodies crashed and rolled but never changed. And I thought I was sinking . . . with waves rushing past high above my head. I awoke in terror. I was sweating like a pig . . . my eyes were out on stalks and I was taking in huge gulps of air . . . but I was no longer stagnant. For there pouring out from me was the story . . . the story of The Ring . . . and it is the story of the dwarfs who crawl the fish that swim the giants that roar and fight and the gods who plot and scheme within me and I tell it to you now so its music may wash through you and clean you out too.

It begins at the bottom of a river.
Water down here is thick like mercury. Silver. Dark.
There is no air.
There is little light.
It is like thick fog down here.
It is very difficult to see more than a few inches in front of your face.
But something is down here. Something is swimming here.
Swimming ever closer, closer, closer.

*

34

What light there is down here catches a glancing blow upon something . . . on one, on two, on three . . . there are three things swimming here. They swirl about . . . they come nearer . . . I can hear laughter. It is three large fish. But they are laughing. They dive, they circle, they laugh. They have faces! They have long, flowing hair. They have the forms of women and they laugh and talk but they are down here at the bottom of the river and they swim like fish. And, Christ, they are playing a game! They are playing Hide-and-seek! They are playing Tag! They are playing Catch Me If You Can!

They are hiding in the murky eddies of the water. There are rocks now. They swim out from jagged holes and their laughter tinkles and guffaws like waves. They are right down here on the bed of the river.

Oh, this river bed frightens. This river bed feels bad.

I don't want to be down here because there is something, or someone down here. There are too many dark nooks and crannies and clefts making this river bed a place of danger. But it is going unnoticed, this feeling, with the three Fish-women.

They are still playing in this deep river, this Rhine, this German river of mine. These Rhine Maidens don't see. They don't see, in their good game they're playing, that something is moving on the river bed! Something is alive, is crawling, is creeping out of a deep cleft, like a maggot out of an apple.

It is walking along the uneven river bed towards them. It is a man, but it is a little man, not full-size, not full-grown . . . it is a dwarf. It is a dwarf coming out of the centre of the earth and out of the very back of my brain and he is walking towards the Rhine Maidens and he is sneaking up on them.

His name is Alberich. He is a Nibelung. He is one of a race of dwarfs who lives under the earth and in the recesses of my head. Nasty bit of business this creature. He is stiff with lust for these Fish-women. He wants them, one of them, any of them, all of them. His desire burns and glows like a firing kiln. He wants the first girl . . . Wellgunde. He follows her. No, he wants the second . . . Woglinde. No, the third, rather. Floss-hilde. He wants to catch one and have her right there on the river bed.

They've seen him! They've spotted him creeping up on them.

They are going to swim, run, dive away!

No, it's another game. It's 'Tease The Dwarf'. They are going to play ball with him. They are throwing him and his Dirty Ideas one to the other.

They are teasing him from rock to rock, they are bouncing him from whirlpool to wave, we are all rising now through the thick swirling water. They let him touch them . . . and then . . . ah . . . they dart out of his bristly, toady clutches. Oh, this is a dangerous game. The Rhine Maidens are wooshing water up his nose. He sneezes, coughs, splutters. He thinks he's going to have one of them. This one, no, that one, no, well, the third. They are playing with him.

He suddenly realizes this. They are calling him ugly, which he is, they are playing with him. Lust is turning into Red Rage now. He is Mad with them. They are playing with Fire.

Somewhere, far above this, clouds part.
The sun comes out.
Its rays stretch like golden slides down, down to the earth.
The light is strong.
It cuts like a sword through the waters of the Rhine, and with the sword's point pricks something on the bed of the river.
It is gold.
I love gold.
It is treasure.
It is all the wealth you have ever dreamed of.
This is The Rhinegold.
This is why I am making music.
With this you are never poor again.

The light of this gold spreads throughout the river water.

Alberich is shaking his clenched fist at the Fish-women.
Then his red-rimmed eyes see the light.
His yellow-cornered eyes see the gold.
'What is that?' he asks.
The Maidens laugh. He knows nothing, this dwarf!
'Why, this is The Rhinegold,' they tell him, 'these are the golden eyes which wake and sleep by turns. Whoever, from this gold, makes himself a Ring, will be blessed with measureless power!'
'Our father told us this,' whispers Flosshilde. She is suddenly cautious. 'He told us to guard it well so that no one can steal it from the water of the Rhine. Be quiet, be quiet,' she whispers . . . but it is too late. The Dwarf knows.
Wellgunde laughs scornfully. 'Oh come on, sister,' she smirks . . . 'you know this gold is safe . . . you know to whom alone it is given to forge this gold!' Woglinde comes near . . . 'Come on, sister, only he who love's power will forswear, only he who love's delight will abjure, only he attains the magic to forge a Ring from the gold.'
    We are OK to be confident about guarding this gold, they think, because whatever lives, wants love. No creature that moves upon this earth would go without love.
Least of all this dwarf who has been chasing us all over the river for this very Thing!

*

But the Nibelung comes from under the earth . . .
and he thinks, well, if I had the gold, I would have
the whole world . . . and his mind and body turn
from the Fish-women to the gold. He climbs, he
darts, he leaps . . . and his tiny hands grasp the
gold!
'Well, well,' he says tearing the gold from the rock,
'I take your gold, I take your light. I will make a
Ring of Revenge from your gold, for, let the water
hear it . . . so I curse love!'
And he's gone, down down to the depths.
Dense night descends.

I think about having a Ring like that.
Oh God.

The music is pouring from me, sweating out my
ill health.
I'm up in the top of my head now.
I want to be somewhere better than river murk,
than muddy Revenge.
Light spreads through the space behind my eyes
and dawn is breaking somewhere on a mountain
top.
Thin golden-red of morning light touches the land-
scape.
Oh, this is a better place to be.
No dwarfs, no fish, no murk of water.
No Ring to tempt me.
My music lights the day.
The Rhine flows far below.

But up here, on this mountain, in peace, lie two figures, fast asleep.
They lie in sweet-smelling flowers.
Wotan, King of the Gods, and beside him, Fricka his wife, Queen.
This is where I want to be.
With Gods.

Oh, and in the distance, as the sun grows brighter, hotter, the farther mountains step forward out of the morning mist and on the highest, steepest mountain stands a fortress.
It is tall, high, beautiful, safe.
Its stone battlements gleam.
It is called Valhalla.
It is the God's new home.

A person might be happy here.
A person might not think of the Ring.

The heat of the sun warms Fricka's face.
She wakes.
She sees the fortress.
She looks at it for a long long time.
Heat on Wotan's eyelids.
His eyes open as he leaves his dreams.
He sees the fortress.
His dreams have become reality.
There it is, his castle in the air.

Inside Fricka is a cold knot the sun cannot warm.

She knows the cost of this piece of building.
Giants toiled long and slow on the jigsaw of stones
that make this castle.
The work does not come cheap.
The cost is high.
The pay packet is her sister Freia, beautiful Freia,
grower of fruit and trees.
She looks at her husband.
'What about Freia? I am afraid,' she says.

Wotan is a God.
He has Power, he has Deceit, he has tricks.
He made the deal, yes, a beautiful fortress for a
beautiful woman.
He gets his dream castle, the Giants get their dream
woman.
Yes, that was the deal.
When Loge, flickering Fire God, dazzling deceiter,
thought it up and talked with tongues of fire,
Wotan had liked it.
Now, he only likes half of it, the half where he
gets the castle.
Now he has sent Loge skittering about the world
to find some way out of this fine mess he's got
Wotan into.
He looks at his wife.
'You wanted me safe and faithful inside a fortress,
Fricka,' he says. 'You want this too. I'm Father of
the Gods. I'll save Freia. Trust me.'

The earth beneath their feet trembles.

Leaves quiver upon their branches.

Something is coming, something heavy, something leaden.

A woman runs into the clearing and although she's frightened, gasping, panting, shaking, the sky brightens, trees shine greener, the grass glistens.

It is Freia, Goddess of Youth and Beauty.

The world gasps at her.

Nature bows down before her.

Her looks, her looks.

The earth rocks and splits, like ice floes shifting and cracking.

Sounds, like a heavy axe striking a trunk of a tree.

It is footfalls.

Freia is running from Giants.

Two colossal figures labour through the trees.

They stop before Wotan.

They point to Freia panting at his feet.

'That is ours,' they say.

The giants Fafner and Fasolt stare with dull hot eyes at their prize, their prey, their pay lying on the grass.

Sometimes I stare at beautiful women and I feel like a dull heavy giant.

Shouting.

Leaping from rock to rock come two fine figures . . . Froh and Donner, brothers to Freia.

They run to pull their sister back, but the giants
push them off with their colossal strength.
Back off boys.
Giants are might.

Wotan places himself between Freia and the Giants.
He has to think fast.
He has to baffle their slow brains, mash their
muddy minds until Loge returns with an answer.
He starts talking to them, twisting their thoughts
this way and that away from Freia, away from
youth and beauty.
They are fixed on her.
They have built a fortress with their big hands.
They can feel the bruises and callouses on their
mighty bodies.
They know this . . . Freia should be theirs.
Wotan's words skid off their domed foreheads.
They want Freia and they want her now . . .

There is a smell of sulphur.
The air flickers blue and yellow.
Everywhere feels dry and hot.
It is Loge, it is God of Fire returning.
A whoosh of heat and he stands before them.
He looks like a man of burning logs.
His eyes glow like coals.
When he speaks there is the snapping of small twigs
combusting.

'Do you want the Good News or the Bad News,' he asks.

'The Bad News, Gods and Giants, is that all the world is good.
Men everywhere agree that there is no higher prize than the love of a woman. So for this finest of fortresses, the highest of prizes . . . the loveliest of women.'
The Giants Fafner and Fasolt reach out their hands to Freia.
Loge puts out a hot hand and draws Wotan aside.
'The Good News, Father of the Gods, is that there is one, only one being who holds a different view. There is someone who prefers gold to girl and he is Alberich and he has stolen the Rhinegold and makes it even now into a Ring . . . perhaps, perhaps . . .' small flames appear in the middle of his eyes . . . 'the stout parties here might like a nice piece of jewellery instead?'

The stout parties aren't having any of it.
They want the woman.
What is a piece of gold after all?
'It is Power, this gold, this ring, Boys,' murmurs Loge, 'and who has this Ring but your old enemy, Alberich, head of the Nibelung. And you know how you hate dwarfs . . .'
Loge's words curl like smoke about the Giants' eyes.

Suddenly, they do not see Freia so clearly.

They see Gold.

They see Power.

They nod their slow shaggy heads.

'We've got them,' flickers Loge at Wotan's ear.

'Now all we have to do is get the Gold.'

Wotan smiles.

He has his fortress, he has Freia.

'How will we get the gold, my bright flame?'

'Well, Father God, the dwarf stole the gold . . . it would only be fair, only be right . . . if we stole it off the dwarf . . .'

'Let us go to Nibelheim,' says Wotan.

Everyone's mouth tastes of ashes.

Wotan and Loge turn to Freia and she is gone.

She is held fast in the calloused hands of Fafner and Fasolt.

They are dull, but not that dull.

Gods are fickle.

They will hold Freia hostage until this Ring appears.

There is many a slip twixt cup and lip when Gods drink tea with Giants.

They pull her away.

She fights and screams, but they are Giants.

As she goes, colours fade, trees start to lose their leaves and the grass turns brown and dry.

The Gods lose their radiance.

Their rainbow auras bleach to white.
Grey appears in their glossy hair.
Lines run and crack in their ruddy complexions.
The Goddess of Youth and Beauty has been taken
from them.
There are no golden apples to keep them young.
The Gods grow old.
The World is Unwell.

We are all losing our radiance.
My music falters.

'To Nibelheim,' says Loge.
'Which way?' says Wotan.
'Through the Rhine.'
'Not through the Rhine. I am cold,' says Wotan.
'Then let's got the hot way,' says Loge, 'let's go
through that sulphur crack!' And like a firework
in the night sky he is light, then he is gone, through
a crevice in the rock.
Sulphur steam fills the air.
Wotan sees the aging Gods.
'I'll get the gold,' he swears. 'I'll keep you young,'
he promises and into the crevice he goes.
The air is hot with sulphur.

I am having another dream.
I am walking through corridors of stone, I am
searching down staircases hewn from rock for
something.
I'm going down again, down into the very pit of

me, my stomach burns, my mouth is dry, my head is pounding.
I'm hot, so hot, I kick the bed covers off.
I'm down somewhere very deep.
My head is pounding.
It's like thousands of hammers beating on my brain.
There's a red light glowing behind my eyes, I can't open my eyes!
Music, HELP ME!

It's the centre of the earth.
A huge subterranean cavern, tunnels leading off everywhere.
Someone is screaming and screeching.
Someone is in pain.
Someone is being dragged along one of the tunnels, these shafts, towards the cavern.
Alberich appears, dragging something.
He has another one of him, he's holding him by the ear.
It is his brother, Mime.
'Where is it where is it where is it?' yells Alberich.
'Not finished not finished not finished!' shrieks Mime.
But something heavy and metal falls from his hands.
And it is finished.

Alberich picks it up.
It is a helmet, forged of gleaming metal.

He puts it on his head and says,
   '*Night and mist*
   resembling nothing!'
And he disappears!
In his place stands a pillar of mist.
'Where are you?' cries Mime in terror.
He looks, sees nothing, but suddenly on his back he feels the lash of a mighty whip, once, twice, three times.
He staggers and screams.
Alberich's laughter rumbles from the centre of the pillar of mist.
'I am everywhere, I am Lord of the Nibelungs, all must work for me and I appear when you least expect me. You are all my slaves!'
And the mist races up and down the tunnels.
Alberich reigns with terror.

Sulphur.
Two Gods emerge from a fissure in the rock.
Wotan and Loge after their gold.
They see Mime writhing and sobbing.
Loge is suddenly all warm fireside concern.
'Mime, little Mime, what's happening?'
And Mime tells him of the horror.
How Alberich has made a yellow ring of powerful magic and he has turned them all into a race of slaves.
For gold for gold more gold gold gold.
'And this is why you are beaten?' asks Loge, his fire warming Mime's tongue.

No, Mime has made a helmet . . . a helmet which
turns the wearer invisible. Wotan thinks the task
of taking the ring will be difficult.
But this is just the kind of game Loge likes.
Loge sits on a stone.
His smile flickers about his mouth.

Alberich arrives in full view, cracking his whip,
driving terrified dwarf Nibelungs back to work.
The dwarfs carry gold and silver and pile it around
the cavern.
The cavern is heavy and gleaming with precious
metal.
Alberich points the Ring.
Terror descends like a black toad.

The Gods mount an attack.
Wotan flatters.
Loge sits and waits.
Wotan admires the gold.
Alberich crows.
'Show me,' says Loge.
    'Giant dragon
    Twist and twine,'
says Alberich.
He disappears instantly.
An enormous dragon appears in his place, writhing
upon the ground, its jaws snapping and biting at
Wotan and Loge.
'Oh, oh, how terrible, how frightening,' yells
Loge, but his mouth smiles.

Alberich reappears.

'Very good,' says Loge, 'but can you do small? Small is more difficult surely?'

Alberich puts on the hat, the Tarnhelm, again.

> *'Crooked and grey*
> *crawl, toad,'*

he says and he becomes a toad.

'Tread on the toad,' murmurs Loge.

And Wotan places his foot upon the toad.

Loge catches its head and removes the Tarnhelm.

Wotan now has his foot on Alberich's neck.

Oh, oh, he's caught!

'Tie him up,' says Wotan.

A rope appears in Loge's hands.

They parcel up the dwarf.

'Let's take him up, he's ours,' says Wotan.

The Gods have won.

The sound of tiny hammers clink and pound as they return, through the mine shafts, past the piles of gold, of silver, through the heat of molten gold up, up into the air.

The music rises and we are on the mountain top once more.

Valhalla glints in the afternoon sun.

'Get the gold, Dwarf,' says Wotan.

Alberich thinks . . . I'll let them have the gold but I'll keep the helmet and the Ring . . . I'll still be powerful.

He calls through the air.

From every nook and cranny Nibelungs scurry
with armfuls of gold so much so much gold.
'Toss the Tarnhelm,' says Wotan.
Alberich thinks . . . I'll let them have the helmet
but I'll keep the Ring . . . I'll still have power.
He throws the helmet on to the gold pile.
'And the Ring, Dwarf,' says Wotan.
No, he thinks, no, no, no, NO, NO!
But Wotan is a God, Father of the Gods and he
takes Alberich's hand and twists the Ring from his
gnarly, knotty finger.
Alberich has nothing now, nothing.
He screams.
Loge says, 'Go home, Nibelung. You are free.'
And Alberich stands and curses.
He calls down a curse on the Ring.
Whoever owns it, he decrees, will never be happy,
never be fortunate, never be free of anxiety, free
of envy.
Everyone will want it, but no one will enjoy it.
Its owner will always dwell in fear, always be a
slave . . . until the Ring is returned to him,
Alberich.

Wotan holds the Ring, turning it over and over in
his hand.
He is now its owner.
Alberich leaps and hops into the crevice.
Down to the bottom of the world, where he will
lie in wait.
For the Ring's return.

*

The air freshens.

The Giants have brought Freia back.

Oh, there's all this gold for them!

But then, they could still keep Freia . . .

she is so beautiful . . .

The Giants say oh, put the gold in front of her, hide her with the gold so we are not tempted by her.

The Gods . . . Donner and Froh . . . Loge . . . Fricka . . . build the gold up around Freia . . . the gleaming wall gets higher, higher.

'I can still see her lovely face,' shouts one.

Wotan throws in the Tarnhelm.

It hides her lovely face.

'I can still see her glinting eye,' say the Giants. 'We want her.'

Only the Ring is left to close up the chink between Freia and the Giants.

'Give us the Ring, Wotan,' say the Giants.

Wotan holds the Ring, turning it over and over in his hand.

He is the owner.

The Power is his.

What shall he do?

He wants to keep the Ring.

It is this Ring I want inside me.

I write my music for this Ring.

Blue intense light, stronger than any other light pierces the air.

A woman appears in it, up from the earth . . .
impossibly . . . and stands before Wotan, she is
brighter than all the gold, all the sun, all the
light . . . she is Erda, Goddess of Earth and Eternal
Wisdom and Eternal Destiny and source of all
knowledge on this world and she speaks:

> '*I know how all things were*
> *how all things are*
> *how all things will be;*
> *A dark day dawns*
> *for the Gods*
> *all that exists will end*
> *I advise you, avoid the Ring,*'

and she returns to earth.
They must heed this terrible warning!
Or it will all continue, all the sickness in me!

It is hard being a God.
Wotan wants the Ring.
But he has been warned by Wisdom.
I know that he and I must give up the Ring!
But oh, but oh, we Want It!
My bowels are water.
My hands shake.
I make the music speak.
He strikes his spear and surrenders the Ring!
The Ring slips like the last piece of a puzzle into
the golden wall.
Freia is free!
Her brothers seize her and pull her into their arms.
Fricka kisses her sister over and over again.

And a shocking change occurs.
The Gods grow younger.
Their hair golds and glosses.
Their skin smooths and reddens.
Their bodies glow with rainbow light.
Youth and beauty have returned to them.

And a shocking change occurs.
The Giants fall to fighting.
Their features set in anger, envy, anxiety.
They are the Keepers of the Ring.
They fight over the gold, so much gold but they fight over it.
They brandish their clubs, swinging them about their heads and aiming them at each other, at their brother.
Fafner connects.
Fasolt's brow splits like a ripe peach.
His head falls into two and blood courses on to the green grass.
The curse is upon them.
Happy Alberich.

Happy Gods.
Valhalla is theirs, youth is theirs, beauty is theirs.
They are going home.
Donner feels the air thick and clammy about him.
He is a God.
He holds a hammer in his fist.

He strikes the rocks.

He holds up his arm and from his fingers forks of lightning beam, thunder cracks.

A storm breaks through the clamminess.

The mist is chased away and there, stretching across to the gates of Valhalla is red orange yellow green blue indigo violet, a rainbow bridge arching over the valley.

The Gods and Goddesses set their divine feet upon the bridge and walk, walk, laughing to Valhalla.

Loge stands, a separate flame, like a street light on the end of a bridge.

He sees the Gods laughing, and he does not laugh.

He sees them joyful and he is not joyful.

He sees their end.

He wants to burn them all up.

And he wants to go with them too.

He steps upon the bridge.

Down below, deep down in the valley there is singing.

The singing sounds like tears, salt and sad.

It is the Fish-women singing about their lost gold.

The Gods hear them.

They take no notice.

They walk into their rainbow fortress.

I feel better.

My head is clearer . . . my skin is smooth.
I've been purged and scrubbed by the music of my story.
But I'm not completely recovered.
I'm in remission.
There's more to come.
It's not over yet.

THE CUNNING
LITTLE VIXEN

Barbara Machin

Based on the opera
THE CUNNING LITTLE VIXEN
Composer and librettist: Leoš Janáček (1854–1928) after a
story by Rudolf Tesnohlidek
First performed: 1924

The trees stand as thick and black as a fence. The dusk comes down like smoke, and somewhere deep in the forest the wind is moaning. From where I stand, the amber headlights of trucks and bulldozers are disappearing one by one, and the men with orange jackets and rusty voices stamp their feet against the cold. They will soon be gone and the trees will flood all their digging with darkness again. A great swathe of our forest has been cut down to build a bright new satellite town for food and petrol fumes. Our frontiers are being drawn tighter around us like a rope.

We're watching and waiting for rich pickings. We rob bins already, of course. We run past the forester's cottage and turn his over, then on to the inn and the village where we crash lids, spill and gorge. And now, as frost bites, saliva freezes on my lips when I think of cooked giblets and chicken bones. These men will bring their gluttony here with them. We've seen it before in the town when we've slunk along tarmac. They'll wheel out bins brimming with strong meat and rancid butter. Children will drop juicy hamburgers half eaten, the meat juices running on the wind. And we'll race down like shadows, returning with tight bellies.

Hunting's not what it was. I'm my mother's daughter, but the world's changing.

The forester understands that too. He stands here every day and stares down on Harasta's buildings like a man watching an earthquake. The businessman's dream was only a plan nailed to a post when my mother was a cub. Marking out the new boundaries and daubing crosses on the trees was the forester's job, but by nights he'd roam the forest with his gun, looking for poachers and hunting for foxes. Which is how he met my mother.

The summer moon was high and white as a bone. Swallowing the night air like strong ale, the forester crouched between the trees with his gun held ready.

'It's gone late again,' he murmured. 'No doubt my wife will be bolting the door against me, and steaming up the windows with all sorts of accusations.' He ran his great red hands along the gun's metalled flank. 'We had good times, her and me, but you're my mistress now, I reckon.' Laughing softly, he put his lips to the shotgun and shrugged down into the bank to wait for poachers. My mother caught his reek of tobacco and sweat as she crept closer. The forester had closed his eyes and was beginning to snore.

The forest stopped holding its breath. Grasshoppers blundered in the undergrowth, and a dragonfly, splendid in flying silks, banked steeply to get a better look. A frog hopped. Green and succulent as a savoury terrine, he glistened near the forester's hand. My mother swallowed hard. Her stomach cramped with hunger, so, inching forward, she pounced.

Feeling slimy feet scud over his face, the forester grabbed at shadows and caught the little vixen's leg. Kicking and snarling, she tried to savage his fingers, but he pulled his leather coat down over her like a moonless night.

'Got you, Bystrouska.' He chuckled. 'Just wait till I show them your wicked teeth.'

He tied my mother up round the back of his cottage. The weekenders used to drive up in their wide wheeled trucks and tramp round to his yard in boots and jackets smelling of fierce new rubber. They'd watch, holding their breath as the vixen sprang at her rope and rolled back her lip in pure hatred. If they got too close they felt the spray of the wild beast on their faces. But the forester would come quietly and sit down on a box. He'd stare, half excited, half mean, like a man in love.

His muscle-bound dog crouched in his kennel. 'Can't stick your stench, vixen,' he growled as she fanned her auburn tail and paced the length of the rope.

'Knucklehead,' she spat back. 'Bog breath.'

The forester's wife sucked in her cheeks and tightened her apron as she put their food down.

'Dear little vixen,' she cooed, 'we'll soon have you tamed.'

'My mother sidled closer and shivered muscles along her back. The woman was reaching out to stroke her when a black mass rose up through her fur and swarmed on to the woman's arm.

'Fleas!' she screamed. 'I'm being eaten alive.'

'Maggot brain,' growled my mother, before glaring at the dog. 'And you're no better, you *poodle.*'

The Rottweiler's stumpy hair stood on end. He whimpered, his eyes flickering. 'You should pity me, vixen. I've never been to your forest, never had a single flea nor a decent fight. Never even been in love.'

The vixen sniffed as the huge dog lapped milk from a bowl. 'I don't know much about love,' she confessed.

'I howl for it, every springtime.' His forehead folded. 'But maybe it's all pig-swill anyway?'

'No . . .' The vixen strained against her rope. 'I've heard it comes like rain. They say it's wilder than weather.' Her eyes glowed like gold. 'I've heard the forest animals talk of it.' She sighed as if to catch the rhythm of the trees in the wind and the dog hauled himself to his feet. His eyes were brighter, his red mouth sagged open.

'Come over here, little vixen . . .' His breath came fast and shallow, '. . . that's not love you're talking about.'

Turning suddenly on the slavering beast, the vixen tore at his shadow with sharp teeth. 'Go back to sleep, punchbag. You've lived too long with men.'

The next morning the forester's son brought a friend to stare at Bystrouska. But she lay there like a cat cleaning her paws with a rough tongue. Thirsty for excitement, they dangled a live mouse by its tail to excite her.

'What a joke,' the city boy jeered. 'She's about as wild as a door-mat.' The mouse smelt my mother stirring like a north gale and screamed with fear, spinning wildly from the boy's fingers. And then Bystrouska leapt. She nipped the creature in a splash of red and sank her needle teeth into the boy's leg.

The forester's wife rushed out and set about the vixen with a soup ladle. 'Punish her,' she screamed. 'Shoot her. You'll never tame a wild beast like that.'

So as darkness fell, the forester marched out into the yard. As he came towards her, my mother recalls it was as if she heard chains at his ankles. He knelt down and cocked the rifle to thumb in cartridges. The sour stench of gunpowder hit the evening air and the vixen shivered and whimpered and crept towards him. Her sleek pelt burned red in the light thrown from the kitchen door and her eyes watched him like water. Nervously he leant out to touch her, and as his fingers sank through

63

her fur, his mind filled with fears of torn flesh and wounding. But she nuzzled willingly into his hands and there was no biting nor blood on his fingers.

'Beauty, Bystrouska,' he whispered, 'and you're all mine.' And with that he tied her harder with a shorter rope with double knots and took his gun back inside.

That night my mother cursed his roped mercy and howled and cried until she dropped with misery. The moonlight flooded around her and as she ached for her freedom, she thought she caught sight of a beautiful girl. Vividly she ran and leapt through trees and sprinted up into the sky. The sudden smell of the pinewood made Bystrouska gulp, and rain washed away the marks where the forester's hand had roughly held her fur. Sharp as a dream, the girl returned to the vixen and placing her arms around her neck, curled against her before falling asleep. By morning she had gone, but the warm weight of her remained round my mother like a harness.

The chickens woke first as always and stupidly strutted about the yard with popping eyes. They gobbled corn and choked on stones and then obediently lowered themselves to strain and push out the morning's quota of eggs. All the while, the rooster posed amongst them like a body-builder.

'Pot-boilers,' chided my mother, 'laying eggs like lackies while all he can do is buff his beak.'

Flexing his pectorals, the rooster crowed indignantly. The hens admired his quivering throat as they always had, and tottered about with admiration.

'You're nothing, vixen,' clucked a maize-fed five pounder, 'why, you can't even lay eggs.' Her fellow chickens thought this hilarious, and cackled with laughter.

'Come and take a look, then?' Mother invited, pacing about hypnotically.

But as the curious chickens darted forward, the rooster ran them back. 'Foxes kill chickens,' he instructed his brood.

'Mass bloody murder,' Mother added under her breath. 'Killing for pleasure, that's what we do to tame things.'

And with that she ran fiercely round in a circle, winding the rope around her neck. 'I'd rather die than let a man rule my life, you battery-brains. Tying me up can't tame me, nor any death.' As the rope pulled tight, she fell gasping to the ground and then lay quite still.

The chickens couldn't contain themselves. They gathered around shivering with disbelief. A bantam with a pedigree silenced them all into awed agreement.

'Personally, I find all this tooth-and-claw stuff too utterly vulgar,' she clucked. 'If God had meant us to be wild, he wouldn't have given us cages.' And with that the vixen leapt and snapped her neck like a twig. Then with jowls bloody and feathered she tore into screaming chickens until their down dropped like snow.

The forester ran at her furiously and wrestling with the rope, unleashed her so he could get a clear shot. Bystrouska, my mother, the cunning little vixen, only remembered leaping at his face and seeing the fear in his eyes. She bit right through to the bone in his hand and as she fled into the dark of the forest she tasted his blood on her tongue like iron.

Bystrouska's return to the wild was a triumph. The animals gathered around her in awe. She had known life as a prisoner and she'd grown wiser. When the badger shuffled out of his hole to reprimand her for unseemly behaviour – for it was not a woman's prerogative to hold court and tell stories – she rounded on him fearlessly. While the forest went quiet and retreated in respect, she squared up to him.

'Things are changing,' she remarked, eyeing his tailored markings and his stance of automatic superiority. 'It's my right to speak. I've earned it.'

'Since when has that had anything to do with anything, vixen?' the badger sneered, as he turned his back on her. The warm harness on my mother's back tightened. Her bravery touched the animals like a forest fire and they rose up angrily against the badger. As he shuffled away, my mother pissed on his doorstep and took over his hole.

Bystrouska started to spy on the forester. She never forgot the chains she had heard on his heels, his hand on her back, nor the look in his eye. Now she curiously hunted that part of him she'd never understood.

One night the forester sat down to drink with his friend the teacher, a weekender. A fierce wind of whisky fumes flooded out of the pub door like a fired trail of petrol. The forester told stories. He talked of floods and frosts, shooting and traps. He grinned at the weekender's soft confidences and his hair cut sleek and straight as a ruled line.

'I've fallen in love with a village woman,' the teacher confessed. 'I only come here to glimpse her. My wife doesn't know.' He sighed miserably. 'Her name's Terynka.'

'Terynka?' The forester grinned. 'But she's taken, my friend. She's married.'

The teacher nodded and morosely gulped down more whisky. Spotting the curate drunkenly listening in the corner, the forester rose unsteadily to his feet.

'Here's to your Terynka, teacher. Here's to your wild passion.'

The teacher shrank into the shadow with shame. His secret had been confessed under solemn conditions and now as it lit up the bar with laughter, he ran away into the night.

'A curse on all womankind,' slurred the curate. 'Hear me well, forester. Even *you* were deceived by no more than a wild vixen.' The forester frowned and brought his scarred fist down on the bar.

The teacher staggered through the forest. He'd never seen such blackness. And then when he struggled into the moonlight the world seemed unreal, without kerbstones. Watching him in the half light, my mother ran her tongue round her teeth. All men were her quarry now.

'Terynka?' the teacher mumbled to himself, more alone in darkness than he'd ever been and with no fear of being overheard. 'Terynka . . .' he called almost boldly. 'At least in this wilderness I can shout your name out loud. Why . . . if I saw you now I'd . . .' He faltered as if he suddenly imagined his wife, his children and his mortgage sliding into the water like an overturned car.

Bystrouska moved pine branches. Cunning as shadow, she mixed her shape and her reds with the moonlight. The teacher saw a girl. 'Beautiful . . .' He stopped and stared. 'Terynka?' He stretched out his hand. '*This* is what the forester boasts about. This place where life is either blood or nothing at all.' He ran forward wildly, his face stretched with drink. 'Terynka . . . I'll have you. I *will*.'

The girl slipped from sight and the teacher only caught a faint reek of fox before he cannoned into a tree and lay like a sack in the pine cones.

Somewhere near, my mother caught the whisky breath of the curate. He was preaching now, missing the path and crashing through the undergrowth. Stalking him silently, the vixen imagined she saw manacles on his wrists, and lead in his pockets.

'Damn her, damn her.' The curate's breath was a flame-thrower. 'Never trust a yellow-haired girl . . . nor any of them.' But then he faltered. In the bushes he could have sworn he saw someone watching. Golden eyes, delicious honey, forbidden fruit, and surely, the shimmer of yellow cascading hair. The alcohol coursed in his blood and he fell to his knees. He gazed into the vixen's golden, melting eyes where without a thought he gave himself up to drowning.

Bystrouska snarled and leapt and suddenly the curate was a man in flight, breath torn like raw flesh from his chest. He ran, leaving a trail of terror scored like footprints in the baked forest floor.

The vixen listened again. Somewhere even more distantly she heard the sound of a shotgun firing blindly into the night. The forester was out searching, angry tears wet on his face. Shivering, she caught his sweat and gunpowder on the air. They were hunting each other.

The next spring Harasta's men started felling trees. A single straight line became a wide scar to mark where the road would run. My mother would lie on this very hill and watch, always wary, tasting the air for danger. Warm on her back and heavier than sunshine she suddenly felt her harness tighten as if the girl were rousing her. Her heart pounded with pleasure and shifting her weight, she saw a young male fox in the clearing. Strong and impatient, he loped against the wind, tracking rabbits, invisible and noiseless as dusk. My mother, Bystrouska, the proud and cunning vixen, fell instantly in love.

A rabbit tore sideways and scuttered across her path. The young fox surged up the hill and stopped dead, struck down with her stare.

'Did I startle you?' He backed off a little to calm his heart, and frowned at the disappearing rabbit.

'Not at all.' Her composure was sudden and sleek.

He watched her boldly, then paced around her, his young pelted body catching the light in a forest of reds.

'There are men nearby,' he announced. 'If you're worried I could walk with you?'

'No need.' She sniffed at his assumption. 'I'm not frightened of men. And I don't need protecting.' From that moment the young fox was caught, and held captive in a glorious circle of excitement. He sat and listened to all she had to tell him, the forester, the dog, the chickens, the taste of iron and her bite through to the bone.

When he left to hunt her a partridge, she closed her eyes in the sun and let the girl on her back run freely. And as she watched her, the vixen called out.

'I love him. They're right. It's wilder than any weather.' She repeated the words again and again until the young fox returned to her side. He'd overheard her and grew bolder. Nuzzling and playfully taking mouthfuls of her fur he threw his warm weight against her and shouldered her to the ground.

'*No!*' she sprang back. '*No.*'

Watching her warily, he could feel a burning where her teeth had closed on him. He could make her regret it. But the thought burnt to nothing like a spark. Besides, there was suddenly something about her which made him still.

'You'll not rush me or chain me.' Her powerful shoulders hunched. 'I'll not stand for it.'

He proved his acceptance by lying silently until the spring day slammed shut and left them with darkness and frost. She made him walk at her side and led him down into the badger hole. Their young passion howled and drew blood. Spring flowers tore open whole weeks early.

'I'm pregnant,' she told him later, her belly swelling. 'We should be married.' The badger spread accusation and as stupid as chickens, the pheasants gossiped and nattered. But my mother, bearing me, my brothers and a sister, faced every woodland creature with pride. They held the wedding party on the day Harasta called a halt to the tree-felling. And into the silence the men had left behind them, the forest ran wild with celebration.

When I first heard this story I wanted to hunt the forester myself and spent young days trying to escape. My mother had lost the need to shadow him now and guarded us day and night. No longer the hunter, it was only when she tore apart the rabbits father brought for us that I saw her murderous quality. Her wildness in me stirred irresistibly.

On just such a day she ripped back fur and locked her jaws and bit through bones. We devoured sweet red flesh whilst she watched over us. And it was she who heard Harasta's fat whistling first and froze as she waited for his smell. Seedy, waxed, and hot with clothing, the squat businessman lumbered towards us. Mother's tail switched. Another smell came: this time, sweat, gunpowder and the flicker of excitement, the forester.

Harasta nudged our rabbit with his new boot and eased the rifle on his shoulder. Frowning at the carcass, the forester glared at him.

'Your property's covered in tarmac, sir, you can shoot what you like down there. But not here.'

Harasta pulled a sandwich out of his bag. 'Just taking a walk, forester. It's your vixen's done the poaching.'

Sweat smeared the forester's forehead as he pulled a fierce metal trap from his bag. 'I've had her once and I'll have her again,' he promised himself quietly. The snare's teeth clanged together, the rusty hinges reeked of death.

Harasta grinned. 'I'd hoped to book a day's shooting with you – for my wedding guests.'

'Getting married?' The forester grinned at the stubby little man in big boots. 'You?'

'Aye.' Harasta waited for the flame to hit the powder. 'To Terynka. She was divorced, you know?'

The forester swallowed hard. Life was a bitter taste, injustice and disappointments. Always wanting more, he too had lusted after Terynka. Life had not been simple. He'd hunted happiness with words and bullets and she'd escaped. Sighing, he cranked the trap into position.

Harasta watched him go and settled down to keep watch. The meat jelly in his pigeon pie inflamed us with hunger. Creeping out into the path, Mother inspected the clumsy steel jaws holding our rabbit. Harasta stirred, and as I inched forward I saw how he watched Mother like a hunting dog.

'*I'll* have her. I'll show that forester,' he muttered, reaching for his gun. 'The vixen's mine. I'll have her made into a muff for Terynka. I'll line it with silk.'

Racing through the leaves, I went to warn her, but she motioned me back sharply with something like murder in her eyes. 'Plunder his picnic bag,' she hissed. 'Leave him to me.'

Bushing her tail, my mother, the cunning little vixen, limped pitifully down the path drawing Harasta and his pigeon breath in zigzags after her. We fell greedily upon his bag, tearing out pie crust and gravy.

If he hadn't fumbled his cartridges, he'd never have spotted us. But as he stooped to pick them up, he turned to see the carnage of his lunch and swung his gun round. My mother screamed, the way vixens can sound more human than animal, and ran towards him. Surely she felt her harness tug and the girl desert her, because she seemed to falter as she drew his gun away from us. The shot echoed forever amongst the black trees but she fell down dead in an instant. I had the taste of gunpowder in my mouth for days.

I hunted the forester grimly after that. He had made this thing happen and there was an old score to settle. A warm weight, a comfort on my back tried to pull me away, but as I crouched outside the inn door I swear I'd have leapt at his throat if I'd heard him happy.

'I still can't believe it.' The schoolteacher in his weekend clothes was dark-eyed with shock and had stopped taking long lonely walks.

'Aye, and did you hear about the wedding, forester?' The innkeeper's wife paused viciously, 'Terynka had the most beautiful fox-fur muff.'

As the forester stumbled out past me I'd have severed an artery in his leg and bit him through to the bone, had he not been blinded by tears. He staggered off towards the forest like a man cut down.

When spring came with all its green and growth, the forest woke again from a long dark sleep. Sitting on this hill, I watched the men down below with a warmth like sunlight on my back. I confess he startled me. His usual print wasn't on the wind and, gunless, he walked slowly, staring like a sleepwalker.

Only when he stopped to push leaves away from the golden aconites did the forester smile. 'Ah me, my wife and I used to come here and make love in the forest. I seem to have forgotten the meaning of spring.'

He sat down only a few feet from me. The hunted smell had gone from him. 'All I want now is forgiveness,' he whispered. And with my mother's name on his lips he closed his eyes.

He slept some while and I lay watching him like a stone until a deliciously green little frog settled nearby. With hunger gnawing at my stomach I pounced, but it escaped and darted away across the forester's face.

He cried out in his sleep. 'Ah, vixen . . . ?' And he grabbed at the air joyfully. But he woke to a little frog wiggling between his fingers. Gently letting the creature go he sat up, rubbing his eyes as if he'd suddenly remembered something.

And then he saw *me*. I faced him proudly,

my red fur blazing in the late sun. He stared for a long time and then smiled as if his hunting was over.

THE MAKROPULOS CASE; KRISTA'S VERSION

In homage to Josephine Barstow, a definitive Emilia Marty

Penelope Farmer

Based on the opera
THE MAKROPULOS AFFAIR
Composer and librettist: Leoš Janáček (1854–1928)
after a story by Karel Čapek
First performed: Brno 1926

My name is Kristina; Krista for short. I'm sixteen years old and in love twice over. First with music – I am a singer. And second with a singer – the singer whom I most want to be. Her name is Emilia Marty. I see her on the stage as often as I can persuade my father to take me. My father is clerk in the law office which is dealing with some lawsuit she's involved in; the Makropulos case, he calls it – it's about somebody's will and doesn't interest me in the slightest. I'm only interested in Marty.

Now please don't misunderstand me; when I say, 'in love' it doesn't mean the way a man is in love with a woman or a woman with a man. I don't want to touch her. I don't want her to turn to me and say 'I love you, Krista,' the way the boy who thinks he's my boyfriend does. No, nothing like that. This love is fierce and hard; like death, you could say. Nothing else in life apart from death swallows you up the way the kind of love I have for music and for Marty swallows me up.

But why do I think of death? Why does some-one my age, sixteen years old, so young, so innocent – 'Little chicken' my father calls me – reflect on death? Because my mother is dead, for one thing. But more because of the way Marty reflects on death; I've seen it; I've heard it. In every role I've heard her sing, she looks at it just as I do, a girl of sixteen, with awe and disdain, with fear and fascination; what's it to do with me? she seems to be saying. I want to be part of Emilia Marty; I want to *be* her – the greatest singer in the world. I want to inhabit her music; for me she is music – really I'm not in love twice over, I'm in love once over; with Emilia Marty; with music – with my own ambition, my boyfriend says, trying to be smart, for once almost succeeding – they say there is wisdom in sorrow. And sorrow is what I bring him.

But my love for Marty will not bring sorrow; my love's not like that. Is it?

Let me tell you about the first time I saw her. It was in the opera house, of course – where else do you fall in love with an opera singer. Even in her dressing-gown, backstage, such glory cannot envelop her so entirely. In a lawyer's office, for all she wafts about in a cloud of perfume, throwing her furs round, making sure everyone knows she is a great lady, she is still just a woman; as Mr Kolonatý, the lawyer, is just a man. This I know from my father. But on stage – where I saw her first as Tosca – heard her sing, so exquisitely, so painfully, 'I have lived for Art and Love' – that's different. That's what I want to live for – and die for – as Tosca died for it. As Marty acting Tosca

80

died; but then came to life again to take her curtain calls. How many times as Tosca, as Violetta, as Mimi, as Butterfly, as Desdemona, has she died and come to life again, I wonder? I know, I've seen her in all those roles. She makes her profession out of them; I have the secret of youth, of eternal life, she seems to say, bowing, smiling, holding out her hands for the flowers that fall about her – I live for ever, her smile says to me, as she opens her arms widely. Even the fall of the red velvet curtain cannot extinguish her, entirely; in my head she still lives on.

Today is the biggest day of my life. My father is Mr Kolonatý's clerk, it is Mr Kolonatý who acts for Emilia Marty in the Makropulos case. And so it is that our tickets for tonight's performance have been given us by none other than Emilia Marty; and that now, the performance over, we are all to visit her backstage. The door in the shabby passage opens. I see her at last, Marty herself, no more or less than I've imagined her, splendid in a gold and scarlet robe, her red hair loose about her shoulders. She has a champagne glass in one hand, she is letting one man after another kiss the other. As soon as I see her, I want to kiss her hand – I want to kiss the hem of her robe – if such a voice was to come from me, I would be happy for ever, I want to tell her. But of course I do not. I am sixteen years old. In my heart I am no age, I am music, I am Marty, I, too, have the voice of a bird which will fill this theatre, every theatre, with the same kind of glory. But it would not be prudent, yet, to show that this is what I think; what I am; what I intend. I stand there meekly with my hands folded, behind my oh-so-meek father, whom I despise for it; who in his turn stands behind his boss, Mr Kolonatý, who not only is a lawyer, he looks like a legal document, long and dry and parchment-coloured; all he lacks is the pink ribbon. He does not kiss Marty's hand. Or rather, he does not intend to do so. But she, seeing us enter, summons him with her hand; he is forced to bow over it, put it to his lips; but does so grudgingly, awkwardly, like a man who is not used to such excesses, and only does so now for the sake of his legal fee. All of which I see Marty observing. I see her appraise each one of those men who kiss her hand – many of them, I can see, want to love her in the way I do not want to love her, as a man loves a woman. One of them – Baron Prus – I know a little; he, too, is involved in the Makropulos suit; he believes he's heir to the estate of a woman who lived a hundred years ago, called Ellian MacGregor.

It's clear from the look in her eye that Marty is no more interested in Baron Prus than the rest of them; and I am glad. At the same time, it's obvious to me, if to no one else, that if he wants something from her – not least her body, the way he ogles her (oh yes, I know about such things; know what she means when she sings 'I have lived for Art and Love') she also wants something from him. Baron Prus, therefore, she plays with a little, letting him hold her hand longer than most, throwing out more than one flirtatious comment. She is acting, I see; she is Tosca again. Tosca wooed Scarpia, to win the life of her lover. I do not think Marty is wooing Prus for any such reason. Whatever it is she wants, it is not that. But she wants something.

I can see my father in front of me twitching with the fear of having to kiss Marty's hand, the way Mr Kolonatý had to. But he is small fry – teasing him is of no interest to Marty. I am resigned to being of no interest to Marty. So far – I am standing a little behind my father, watching her, learning how to do it – I don't think she's even noticed me.

But suddenly she does notice me. I observe it happen. I observe the interest in her eye; this I do not understand, not in the slightest. Suddenly she summons me. As I move reluctantly towards her, I see her call Mr Kolonatý back. Though she speaks to him in a whisper, I can read her lips; it's one of the useful skills I do not admit to having. She is asking, 'Is that your daughter?'

I cannot see Mr Kolonatý's lips. But I see him shake his head. Of course. I am not his daughter, though sometimes I wish I was. The head of a legal firm can afford better singing lessons for his daughter than a mere clerk, like my father.

Now I am close to Marty. I see the powder

on her cheeks; the greasiness of her lipstick; the running of her mascara. I see the lines round her eyes – she is much older than she looks at a distance; but never mind, I am not disappointed; it's how she looks on stage, how she sings that matters; also her being a beautiful woman – even with the lines and the powder and running mascara, I hold my breath at her beauty. But she is asking – she is asking *me*, directly:

'And how old are you, darling?'

I can hardly get my voice out; I have to use my voice training to project the sound from my chest. I wonder if she notices that's how I do it – if she sees that I, too, am a singer?

'Sixteen,' I say. 'I'm sixteen, Miss Marty.'

'Sixteen. Sixteen,' she repeats, and sighs. Then she waves her hand – 'I want to talk to this girl,' she says, making me think for one glorious moment that she sees into my heart, my future; one genius recognizing another. 'The rest of you,' she demands, 'get out. Leave us'. And to my astonishment, they do leave us. I see my father gesturing to me. I know why he is so anxious; he's afraid I'll say something to disturb her business at Mr Kolonatý's office; and that if so he'll be blamed for it. I feel a flicker of pity at such anxieties – in spite of everything I love my father, he's good to me; he buys my lessons. But a moment later I care about nothing; except this; that it is her and I; Marty and Krista; like conspirators on the one hand, competitors on the other; staring deep into each other.

I find my breath at last. I am about to burst out, 'You know – you know I am a singer. Teach me. Help me.' Too late. Because Marty gets in before I do – obviously she is determined to do so. This is my first lesson; Marty is not interested in me, in that way. She hasn't even asked my name, has she? She does not want a happy little chat, teacher to protégé, let alone genius to genius. What Marty wants is to talk about herself – at least to start with. Maybe the rest will come later, I think, as she puts her hands up to stop me speaking. Well, I am patient; I have my life before me; I can wait. And anyway, why should I mind, I am flattered, that it is me, Krista, sixteen years old, to whom the great Emilia Marty has, for the first time, chosen to tell her story; her life story.

Let us be quite clear, though; here is the mystery. It does not seem straight off to be her life story. It starts over three hundred years ago for one thing, in the sixteenth century, and it's about someone called Elina Makropulos; not Emilia Marty.

Before she begins, Marty sinks back on to the chaise longue at one end of the dressing-room. She waves me to sit at her feet – I have to turn sideways to see her face, not a posture I can sustain for long; maybe that's why she insists on it. It means that for much of the recital, I hear her voice only. I suck the little violet sweets she has handed to me; at times I almost faint in the heat of the room, the stink of flowers. You have to appreciate that Marty is wearing a négligé merely – sometimes when I turn to look at her its gold and scarlet silk has fallen away a little, giving me a glimpse of white throat, of long leg, before she adjusts it. I, on the other hand, am wearing my winter coat; not wanting to interrupt the voice, I daren't remove it; I am sweating.

Let me explain also, in advance, how the voice changes; while she tells the story, Marty plays as many parts as she plays on stage. One minute she's coarse as a street woman, calling me 'ducky', the next I'm her 'darling', the next she's a grand lady, addressing me as 'child'. 'Well, ducky,' is how she begins. 'Well, ducky, this Elina's old man, her father, he was a doctor; physician to the Emperor Rudolph II, no less. Now what's your idea of a doctor, darling? A man in a white coat, bit full of himself, not the least interested in philosophy? So what's he good for then? Doesn't attempt to banish death does he – or only till tomorrow. Whereas Elina's dad, darling – *he* did; he tried to banish death. For he wasn't only a doctor; he was an alchemist – a magician of sorts. He tried to make gold – oh yes he did, ducky – he tried to unravel all the secrets of the universe, of life and death, of good and evil. Wasn't no magician to match him – or no one *I* knew of.'

Marty's voice rings out proudly here. There is no one to match her, either, I think, twisting to look at her, dazzled by the fires of her red hair, her black eyes. Was this an ancestor of hers? Does she claim him? But now Marty is talking about the girl; Elina Makropulos. And once that name comes up, the way she talks of the father changes also. I look at her again then, but carefully; she is still not looking at me. At this moment she scarcely seems to know I am there. She is staring towards the mirror at the back of the dressing-table; the very dressing-table at which she must sit to make up before she goes on stage. Little light bulbs edge it – the boxes of greasepaint are all open – so have I been staring at them, knowing that this is what I want for myself, the bulbs, the greasepaints, the notes from admirers pinned up all round, the shabby plush on the dressing stool, the flowers crammed into vases – oh, the scent of lilies that fills this room. I will never smell lilies again, I think, without seeing in my mind's eye, Emilia Marty, just as I see her now; her reflected image framed by lilies and little lights, behind her a darkness in which I am or should be – but I cannot see myself. On her the soft light abolishes the signs of age, I've noted. It does not make her look young, exactly; it makes her as ageless as a woman in a portrait painted centuries ago.

How does she see herself, I wonder – *if* she sees herself; for, all the time, she is looking at something in the shadows behind her. There is hatred in her voice now; or if not hatred, great rage, great bitterness. She is explaining how the girl didn't know her mother, her mother was dead; she only knew her father, or rather she knew her father's arts, because he used her as his apprentice; he needed to pay *her* nothing, said Marty, angrily. She had to grind powders, cleanse beakers and retorts, watch the cauldrons seething with his concoctions ('how they *stank*, ducky') and so on. Sometimes, worst of all, she had to assist him in the rituals by which he called up the powers of the earth and the heavens; the spirits of the deep; the spirits of the dead. But in those cases, always, she had to turn her back; to feel such things behind her back, to hear them, was worse, Marty says ('How much worse you can't imagine, darling,') than being allowed to see them.

The alchemist never managed to make gold, to the Emperor's disappointment; he'd hoped all along that Makropulos would make him rich. But when Elina was sixteen, he did make an elixir of life; now His Imperial Highness could live for ever, he said to his employer, unlike his lowly subject.

The Emperor was in a foul mood that morning. He said, 'how do I know you're not trying to poison me, you old rogue?' (or words to that effect). Adding that, if Makropulos wanted to demonstrate good faith, he should be willing to try the elixir on someone who meant something to himself, before inflicting it on his master.

'My daughter, for instance?' asked the magician, Makropulos.

'Your daughter? Why not?' repeated the Emperor.

Marty pauses, at this point in her story. She raises herself off the bed, leans down, drags me by the hand; grips me; I want to cry out; but I cannot. Far from refusing to look at me now, she is gazing pitilessly into my face; spitting the words at me. 'Now do you see, darling? Now do you see? And how do *you* rate a daddy who values his fee, his reputation, above his darling daughter? You think I had a choice in the matter? You think wrong. It's not the same for you. These days, girls like you get a choice; you can tell Daddy what you want and expect to get it. But I didn't. When my daddy handed the bottle to me, I obeyed him. I drank, meekly.' She burst out laughing then, mirthlessly. So did I burst out laughing at the thought of Marty doing anything meekly.

'But I will tell you this, darling. Elixirs of life aren't meant for sixteen-year-old girls. Elixirs of life are for the old and weary who know the value of life and death. But how was I supposed to know? Go on, tell me. My father gave me the liquid – it was in a green bottle – it tasted of . . . horses. I drank. At his command, I drained it. And that was that, ducky, as the mosquito said to the racehorse.'

At what point I take in the change of pronoun, from 'she' to 'I' I cannot be sure. Even before I take it in, the story holds and disturbs me still more than the story of Tosca does when Marty sings it. I pity the girl, Elina; at the same time I envy her. Since the death of my mother, I awake screaming in fear sometimes from dreams of death. The thought of having that fear, those dreams, taken away from me seems so good, that what it means to Marty I cannot feel for a moment; I cannot think.

She is hissing at me again; gazing at me with those black eyes of hers, swallowing me up. 'Can't you see, child, what I am telling you?'

And still at first I do not see; maybe I dare not. How can I let this woman hold my hand, look into my head, and know that I touch, I see, am seen by, am addressed as child, as ducky, as darling, by a woman who's lived for more than three hundred years?

'Elina Makropulos,' Marty is saying – or rather, chanting. She chants all these names, twice over. 'Ellian MacGregor. Eugenia Montez. Elsa Muller. Ekaterina Myshkin – Elina Makropulos. I was all of these, ducky – you can't keep one name for three hundred years, can you? Not dying's an aberration, just like madness and epilepsy; you keep quiet about it, you have to.' (Staring at her in horror, I see why you must keep quiet.) 'But now I am—' and here she pronounced it, sonorously, like a sentence of death: 'I am, darling, the great, the only, Emilia Marty.' And as she pronounces her sentence, I can, despite my horror, deny the thing no longer.

I spring back from her – to my feet – in pity and fear, and longing. Pity for Elina Makropulos at this moment more than for her, Marty – it is hard, still, to take in that they are one and the same.

Marty throws back her head and laughs again, very loudly. 'Think of it, darling. Think of all that glory all those years. At every curtain, Tosca rises again; lives for ever. The flowers fall about her. The voice never dies. Think of it, darling. Don't you envy me? Don't you?'

But she is not talking to me. She is talking to herself. And now I see how, after all those years, she can talk to no one but herself. She has seen too many of us come and go; her father, her family, her children, her friends, her lovers. What is she left with after all these years, these centuries, but herself, Marty?

Perhaps I grow up in that moment; gazing into the frigid and hollow eyes of someone who cannot see me, because she has lost the power to see me. For her I might as well be – I am – herself, Elina Makropulos, sixteen years old; whom she can no longer reach, no longer touch, not even in me, sixteen-year-old Krista – who, I have to admit, in the beginning, saw her, not as herself, but as my future. But who now dare not, cannot, look on her as anything but herself.

She is not laughing any longer. 'My time's running out,' she hisses. 'So is the elixir.' Seeing the lines gathering round her eyes, I want to scream but cannot. When I turn desperately away and gaze into the mirror framed by little lights, there is no one there any longer. 'The formula is my only hope, darling. My father wrote it down, how to make the bloody stuff. I left the paper to Ferdy Makropulos my son – Ellian MacGregor's son. Now Baron Prus has it – don't ask me how – it's a long story; he'll give it to me, in return for a favour. And when he does, I will give it to you. Read it. Make up the mixture, take it – or give it to me. Or don't read it; burn it. It's up to you. I've had to wait three hundred years to make my choice. You've got yours now, ducky,'

Maybe she has not only the elixir – the remains of it – in her body; maybe she also has her father's magic. As if to make clear to me what I am choosing, she proceeds to show me in herself, the sixteen-year-old Marty – Elina Makropulos. I see the smooth cheeks and clear eyes that in me I take for granted; I see the lithe body, like my own. But even as I watch, the girl fades into the woman, the one I want to be, who sings 'I have lived for Art and Love', who dies, nightly, and at the rising of a velvet curtain returns to life – who could wish for such a life to end? Not I, I think, hearing in my head that glorious voice; replacing it with my own. For I, too, I know in this moment, could be, am, in years to come will be, an Emilia Marty. I am weak with my ambition.

But she does not see; at no point does she see me. She is too old for that. And even as I watch, she becomes old before my eyes, her skin withers, her eyes retreat into her head – her teeth – she has no teeth; suddenly she is toothless. The leg I see inside her gold and scarlet robe is shrivelled. The red hair turns white. A huge ring slides from her emaciated finger, clatters at my feet – I gaze at it, horrified, I dare not pick it up. In less than a minute she has turned from Elina Makropulos, sixteen, like myself, to the prima donna, Emilia Marty, and from thence has become ancient; a bare-gummed, mouthing crone; for that's how I see it; leaving death as the only option.

I scream; I snatch my hand from hers. She is asking me to choose *that*? That my perfect flesh, will turn to *that*? Against an elixir of life; of eternal youth? The choice I'm offered is as cruel as the choice she was not given. Giving me no more quarter than her father gave her, she replaces his cruelty, ambition, his subservience to his master with her own. I am as much a victim as she was; for how can a mere human be expected to make such a choice? The realization of what we are, must come to, is one thing; to be shown it so starkly, at such an age, as if on your own body, is another.

When Elina's father conjured such spirits, he made his daughter turn her back on them; me, Emilia Marty forced to stare them in the face.

Hadn't she said to me herself, I think, that this is no choice for girls of my age? I know what she means now. Of course I will not burn the formula, I start to say, angrily; how can I burn a secret that can save me from – *that*? Meaning what she'd turned into; which I cannot even bear to look at any longer.

But when I do turn my eyes back, she is Emilia Marty again; the crone is only to be seen in the lines around her eyes and mouth. I look into her eyes; as she looks into mine, forcing me deep, deep, inside her. I see nothing there of love or pity. I see only a coldness, like gazing up at the stars on a dark night, into the vastness of a universe in which human feeling is too small, too meaningless, to live. Again, I feel creeping into me a pity for this woman, in all her incarnations; as Elina Makropulos; Ellian MacGregor; Eugenia Montez; Elsa Muller; Ekaterina Myshkin; Emilia Marty. It is pity rather than fear decides me; as it is also a sense that she and I are connected, and not just by the ambitious love, the love of ambition, which she first aroused in me. We, she and I, are making this decision together; in my decision lies hers, also.

When I look at her again, I observe for the first time – I do not think it is an illusion, though it might be – that now she is reading me; that, now, she sees me. She smiles – only briefly; but I catch it, I feel, because I need to feel, that I and Elina Makropulos, are, for a moment, sixteen together.

'What is your name, darling?' she asks me, at last. And when I tell her, she goes on, 'Well, Krista darling, Krista ducky, what's it to be?' I take her hand in mine, then drop it. I smile. I'm not too afraid now to pick up the ring that fell to the floor – it is a yellow stone, I notice, a topaz, in a gold setting. Laying it in the palm of the hand she holds out to me, it is as if I affirm our contract, our joint decision. 'Have you made up your mind, Krista?' she urges. This time Krista answers: 'Yes, Elina.'

SOME GREAT STORMFOWL

Dennis Hamley

Based on the opera
DIDO AND AENEAS
Composer: Henry Purcell (1659–95)
Librettist: Nahum Tate, after Virgil
First performed: London 1689

HENRY PURCELL

The poet wishes well to the divine genius of Purcell and praises him that, whereas other musicians have given utterance to the moods of man's mind, he has, beyond that, uttered in notes the very make and species of man as created both in him and in all men generally.

Have fair fallen, O fair, fair have fallen, so dear
To me, so arch-especial a spirit as heaves in Henry
    Purcell,
An age is now since passed, since parted; with the
    reversal
Of the outward sentence low lays him, listed to a
    heresy, here.

Not mood in him nor meaning, proud fire or sacred
    fear,
Or love or pity or all that sweet notes not his might
    nursle:
It is the forgèd feature finds me; it is the rehearsal
Of own, of abrúpt sélf there so thrusts on, so throngs
    the ear.

Let him oh! with his air of angels then lift me, lay me!
    only I'll

Have an eye to the sakes of him, quaint moonmarks,
    to his pelted plumage under
Wings: so some great stormfowl, whenever he has
    walked his while

The thunder-purple seabeach plumèd purple-of-
    thunder,
If a wuthering of his palmy snow-pinions scatter a
    colossal smile
Off him, but meaning motion fans fresh our wits with
    wonder.

GERARD MANLEY HOPKINS, 1879

'This is the end of the Northern Line. We are at High Barnet station.'

I stood on the platform, perplexed. My guide saw my confusion.

'Yes, it is strange,' the indistinct figure in the semi-darkness continued. 'Being on High Barnet station is to enter another age. Look at the roofs over the platforms. All those ornate white finials hanging down like wooden icicles. There should be steam engines here, not silver tube trains.'

I was still bemused. My guide continued.

'If you really want to see what the age we have arrived in is like, you have to go to Cock-fosters, just along the road. Where the Piccadilly Line ends. All glass and concrete. Very different.'

What was I doing here? I was still shaken, as if the victim of a violent press-gang. But I had been dragged far further than to the deck of any ship of the line. One moment I was sitting, pen in hand, working on a new ode (for I do *so much* want one day to be Poet Laureate) as I passed the afternoon before that evening's important engagement; the next, the same spectral figure now pointing out inexplicable sights had appeared beside me from nowhere.

'You must come on a journey with me, Mr Tate.' His voice was dry, like dead leaves. 'There are things you must be made to think about. You may have over-reached yourself in what you have tried to do. But perhaps it is not too late. There is one whom you must meet. I have arranged an encounter on neutral ground.'

And before I could take breath, we were away, passing together through the very bowels of the earth, across chasms and down precipices, wordless shrieks from who knows who echoing in our ears, epochs and aeons consumed in the twinkling of an eye – to this place.

'Time to leave you, Mr Tate,' said my guide. 'For the moment, anyway. A safe journey to you. And an informative one, I hope. That's your train, over there. When you have boarded, you will know where to go.'

He lifted a gaunt arm which pointed darkly at the next platform. So the line of lighted windows constituted this 'train'.

'You must fight your way home at teatime

through the crowds of typists. So many, flowing round you. I had not thought . . .'

And he was gone. I was alone in the dusk, except for those chattering masses of alien people pushing past me out of the station. The train my guide had indicated stood empty and waiting to leave. I stepped off the platform into a coach half-way along and sat down. I was alone, in silence, cut off from the time-ridden world outside.

Someone had left a broadsheet on the seat opposite, open at a page headed 'What's On?' An advertisement caught my eye. There was a performance that night in the Purcell Room on the South Bank. Ah, yes. Henry Purcell. Sounds of cool strings, tinkling harpsichords and soaring voices in harmony filled my mind.

Of course, I thought. That is where I am going. My guide was right. I leave the train at Waterloo.

The train started smoothly and pattered along the tracks.

'This train has much further to go than Waterloo, and I go with it all the way,' said a voice.

I looked to my left. A man sat there – I had not heard him enter. Had he read my thoughts? His face was oddly familiar – a compound of many I seemed to know. His baked features and dusty cloak spoke of far lands and distant skies. His deep-set eyes, I knew at once, had seen sights known to few.

I looked at the map of the Northern Line above the window.

'You mean to Morden?' I said.

He ignored me and continued. 'And I could tell you such tales of what has been and is still to come.'

'So could I. I tell tales as well.'

Was I his rival, that I spoke so? Yes, I was. Anger rose in me. Was I not Tate? In the telling of tales and writing of epics, was I not supreme? Had I not improved the low-born Shakespeare's *King Lear* and made the ending fit for gentlefolk to watch? Was it not I who had rid the Psalms of David of nonsense and made them rhyme so artisans could understand?

Yes I had, and yes it was. And now I sat on this tube train berated by a swarthy stranger who had read my thoughts. If he could do that, then he *must* know who I was, yet still he went on.

'Arms and the man, I sing. I give you quests and destinies. Of duty, which overrides every other thing. Of the gods and their inscrutable purposes. Of great love and passion. Of betrayal. Of necessary and terrible death.'

'So do I,' I said. He wasn't having it all his own way.

He stood up. As when a sable cloud bearing rain and thunder disfigures the face of the sun and bars its light from beseeching man, so now his darkened visage glowered at me.

'I know you for a nonentity and a dull fellow.'

Know me? How could he know me? I didn't know him. And, because of where I was, I didn't even seem to know myself. But again I felt there *was* something about that lean, keen face which stirred recollection.

'I know you for a teller of small stories, shallow stories, *silly* stories. Mine range over oceans, whole worlds – yea, through the heights of heaven and the depths of hell themselves.'

I had to be impressed. 'Big ones, then,' I said.

'And what do *you* do?' The contempt in his voice was cavernous.

By comparison with that, what indeed?

As the train stopped at Totteridge and Whetstone, the doors slid open and no one got on, my mind stayed a blur. So much, then, for my many great achievements. But this person befuddled me.

'You shout so loud I can't think.'

'You cannot think because there is no passion in you,' said the man. 'If there is no passion, there can be no stories.'

'I can tell of passion,' I replied.

'I mean the passions of the great. Gods. Princes. Queens.'

'Them as well.'

'Very well, tell me a story of grand passion with a queen and a prince in it and I will tell you one. Then we shall see.'

It was a challenge. I would rise to it.

'Well,' I said, racking my brains. 'What queen would you like? Eleanor? Elizabeth? Mary? – I mean the one married to William of Orange. She's the queen I know best.'

'I know none of these queens.'

Pity. I could cobble together a story about them all right, if I put my mind to it. Enough to show this presumptuous hack.

'All right. What queens do you know?' I said.

'The greatest of all, who could have ruled the world. Tell of Dido, Queen of Carthage.'

Of course. I knew *all* about Dido, Queen of Carthage. How could I forget her? A whole story seemed to come into my mind as if it had been waiting to be called. Had I written it already? Or was I about to?

'That was a long time ago,' I said.

'TELL IT,' he thundered. 'And I will compare your story with mine, for I too have told it.'

'Don't get agitated,' I said.

I let the train leave Finchley Central before I started. I had to compose myself before reaching back so many thousands of years.

'Well, one day, Dido, Queen of Carthage sat in her palace surrounded by all her courtiers and servants wondering what to do. They were all telling her she should marry this Trojan Prince called Aeneas, who had turned up one day when his ships bound for Italy were blown off course in a storm. Dido wasn't sure, but all the courtiers were, especially her attendant, Belinda. Aeneas had told them he had escaped from—'

'Who?'

'Who what?'

'Dido's attendant. Who?'

'Oh, her. Belinda.'

'*Belinda?* There was no one in Carthage called *Belinda.*'

Her name could have been 'woodlouse' judging from the scorn in his voice.

'How do you know?'

'Anna. Her sister, Anna, *that* was who Dido confided in.'

'Well, anyway, Aeneas had told her all about how the Greeks had captured Troy with the wooden horse and how he and the other survivors had managed to get away and were looking for a new land to settle in. And Belinda—'

'Anna.'

'*Belinda* said that Carthage and a new Troy together would be invincible so she ought to marry him. And everybody could see that Dido fancied him so why not, she said.'

The man's face seemed to have gone mauve.

'And then Aeneas came in. "When, Royal Fair," he says, "Shall I be blest?" And she doesn't know still, so he says, "If not for mine, then the Empire's sake." When I think of it, that Aeneas really was a two-faced bastard.'

The man stood up. His face had changed from

mauve to deep purple. He looked as though he could strangle me.

'You speak of the greatest Trojan of them all. He is the deliverer of his people. He is the founder of Rome. He is the man of destiny. He is the child of the gods.'

'He was a pain.' And I meant it.

There was a hissing noise as if a boiler was about to burst – and it was nothing to do with the train.

'Pity he turned up at all,' I went on. 'Poor Dido need never have known him.'

'The gods brought him.' The hissing sound had come from the man, but judging from the way he was speaking through clenched teeth, his boiler wasn't going to burst – yet . . .

'Jove himself stirred up the storm to blow him to the coast of Carthage,' he roared. 'Venus, the Goddess of Love herself, was Aeneas's mother, and she wanted Dido to fall in love with Aeneas's son, Ascanius. But such was the power of the words Aeneas spoke as he told of the flight from Troy that Dido fell in love with him instead. Aeneas alighted on the African shore out of the god-given tempest like some great stormfowl, and Carthaginian wits were fanned in wonder at the sight of him.'

That, to me, sounded ridiculous.

'Anyway,' I continued, 'while Dido was still making her mind up, everybody left the palace and went off to the hills and the vales, the rocks and the mountains, the musical groves and the cool shady fountains.'

'Did they indeed?' said the man.

'Yes,' I said firmly.

The boiler was plainly hissing again as he spoke next.

'I bring Aeneas at the behest of the gods through gales, across tumultuous oceans to a woman who, with him, holds the destinies of whole peoples in her hands, and you send them for a walk in the country?'

'Why not?'

'Go on.' A note of weariness had crept in.

'Well, there was this cave full of witches. All right, wayward sisters, if you want to be pedantic. They didn't like Dido because she was too well off. "The Queen of Carthage whom we hate as we do all in prosperous state." That's what they said about her.'

'What have these wayward sisters got to do with it?'

'They're going to upset her. They're going to play a trick on Aeneas so he thinks he's got to leave Carthage whether he likes it or not, so Dido will be left on her own. Wretched by sunset, that's how they want her.'

As I was speaking, the man's face changed. The hissing stopped; he was now deathly pale and he was beating his head rhythmically against the window. The train had left Tufnell Park before he could turn his haggard visage to me.

'Look,' he said in a voice of tired patience. 'The history of the then known world turned on whether Dido married Aeneas. Any tricks were played by the gods themselves. These are epic events you are dealing with. Nothing to do with a few jealous old crones.'

'But you must admit it's pretty clever how they fool Aeneas.'

'Amaze me.'

'The chief witch makes her attendant elf look like the god Mercury so Aeneas thinks the message from the gods is really genuine.'

'Wrong. Aeneas was told to leave by the *real* Mercury. Shall I tell you why? The great Jove himself thought that for Aeneas to marry Dido and build his new city in Carthage would ruin his plans for Rome, so he sent Mercury with the message.'

I ignored him. 'But before that,' I said, 'the witches start a storm.'

'No,' he thundered. 'Your version is a travesty. The storm was started by Juno, Jove's wife, because she wanted Dido to marry Aeneas. They take shelter in the cave and there they cement their love.'

It was my turn to stare. 'Cement? What do you mean, cement?'

'Do I have to spell it out?'

'I think you'd better.'

'I shall have to use the sort of language for this that you seem to favour. What do you think they did in the cave? What would any man and woman who find they are madly in love do, if they were stranded alone in a cave during a storm?'

Now I was indignant. 'There'll be nothing like that in any story of mine,' I said. 'Dido's love was pure and noble and tragic. I won't have her name sullied by such filth.'

'The Aeneas you picture wouldn't be capable of it anyway.' He smiled slightly. For the first time he seemed to show a little sympathy. And, as we left Camden Town, I began to warm to him as well, this grave stranger given to anger but with hints of a greatness which might well outstrip my own.

'Continue with your story,' he said.

'Now they're all out in the country. They all say how nice it is in the grove and how it's just like the place where the goddess Diana hunted and where Actaeon was torn to pieces by the hounds for watching Venus bathing.'

'Better.'

'And Aeneas has killed a huge boar and stuck its head on the end of his spear. The head is so big and heavy it makes the spear bend.'

'I like that,' said the man. 'Actaeon died because of his own weakness. Aeneas has found the greatest prize in the hunt and killed it. Both of these things prefigure what is to happen to Dido. Not bad, not bad at all.'

I began to warm to his approval. 'Dido notices the sky is black. There's a storm coming. She says they must all leave the open fields and go back to town. So they go.'

'Just like that.'

Obviously I had stopped impressing him. 'Well, they've got to be quick.'

Mornington Crescent.

'And then what?'

'Aeneas is left on his own and the witch's elf disguised as Mercury arrives and tells him that Jove says he's got to go that night. And Aeneas says he will.'

'Just like that.'

People who repeat themselves are unsure of their ground. Perhaps I was getting the better of him.

'Well, he's got to reach Italy and rebuild Troy.'

'Isn't he sorry?'

'Of course he is. But he says it's all the gods' fault, so nobody can blame him.'

'Just like that.'

'Stop saying that.'

'But I do not see how the Aeneas in your version can be the great Prince and leader who was the child of the gods and founded Rome. He's not the Aeneas I know.'

He was angry again as the train slid into Euston.

'I can't help that,' I replied. I felt quite confident now with this strange visitor. 'I said he was a two-faced bastard. By their deeds shall ye know them. What people are is what people do.'

'Not entirely.'

'Anyway, Aeneas goes off, the witches do a quick gloating dance and then the sailors start loading the ships. They've been having a great time in Carthage, but the leading sailor tells them to take a short boozy leave of their women, and they can promise whatever they like because thèy'll none of them be back, ever.'

'How honourable of them,' said the man.

'Well, you know what sailors are,' I said.

'No better than Aeneas, according to you.'

True. I hadn't thought of that.

'Then the witches come and watch the ships being loaded and have another good gloat. "Our plot is took, the Queen's forsook," they say.'

He winced.

'Then Dido, who knows that Aeneas has gone off her, tells Belinda that there's no use asking the god to help because it's they who've got her in this mess.'

'I thought you said it was a few witches.'

I ignored him and waited till Tottenham Court Road had faded behind us.

'So there's only fate itself she can trust in.

Then Aeneas comes in and when he says he doesn't know how he's going to tell her, she says not to bother. He's cheated her, saying the gods have told him to go. "Thus hypocrites that murder act make heaven and gods the author of the act," she says.'

'Strong words.'

I looked at him sharply. If that was a compliment, it was very unexpected. Was he making fun of me?

'Anyway, Aeneas says he'll stay after all. Dido says that's no good, he should have said so at once. So he goes, and she dies.'

'How?'

'Of a broken heart.'

'You mean Aeneas goes and she lies down and dies?'

'Of a broken heart.'

'Just like that?'

Fourth time.

'Why not? This great, pure, noble love of hers, ruined by that wretch – I'm not surprised.'

Leicester Square came and went. My inquisitor stood up. But he was not preparing to get off at Charing Cross. He was about to hold forth again.

'Now I shall tell you what really happened. Dido was so stricken by what she thought was Aeneas's treachery that she resolved to commit suicide. Aeneas didn't decide lightly about what to do: he agonized over it. But he was just a counter in a great plan being worked by the gods. This was of no consolation to Dido, who ordered that all the possessions of Aeneas that were left behind were to be put into a huge pile to be burnt, with an effigy of him on top, lying on his bed, so that no trace of him would remain. Nobody had any idea that this was really Dido's funeral pyre. Meanwhile, the Trojan ships left under cover of darkness to avoid a battle with the Carthaginians. And when, next morning, Dido woke to find Aeneas had slipped away, she climbed to the top of the pyre and, lying on the bed next to the effigy of Aeneas, killed herself with the very sword he had once given her. She fell on its sharp point, blood soaked the funeral pyre and Anna grieved over her as she slowly died.'

I listened politely to this ridiculous rigmarole. Now was my chance to really assert myself. After all, I was good with endings. Look what I did to *King Lear*. What he had just said was nearly as bad as having Cordelia die.

'Dido died of a broken heart,' I repeated. 'And little cupids came and scattered rose petals over her.'

As we stopped at Charing Cross I could see he was getting angry again. So I spoke very quickly.

'And as she died, she said, "Remember me, but ah! forget my fate." '

'Say that again.'

He really was strange, this fellow. His anger had disappeared the moment it came. His voice had taken on a note of real interest.

' "Remember me, but ah! forget my fate." '

'Ah.' He repeated the words wonderingly. 'That's good. I'll forgive you a lot for that line. It sings.'

'What do you mean, "It sings"?'

He didn't answer. He just gave me a look which seemed to have something in it I didn't want at all. Pity. I should have kept my big mouth shut and glowed for a second or two in his praise.

'Well, that's it.' I said lamely. 'That's the story.'

The man stood up. He looked down on me from a great height. His voice, when it started, wasn't angry – just very, very sad.

'You have turned one of the greatest stories ever known into a trivial encounter between a virgin and a fool. I tried to put you right but you took no notice. Whenever I have detected a strength in your story, you do not seem to understand what I mean. I despaired of you. But then, at the very end, you sum up the whole thing so beautifully. "Remember me, but ah! forget my fate." I wish I had written that.'

I stared at him long enough for the train to leave Embankment and burrow under the Thames.

'I get off at Waterloo,' I said. 'On the other side of the river.'

'Where did you go wrong?' mused the man.

'Why could you not encompass the heights and depths of your story? Why has the great stormfowl not landed on your shore and fanned your wits with wonder?'

'Eh?'

'You must remember that I likened Aeneas landing on the shores of Carthage to some great stormfowl alighting on the beach. And so he was. Alas, those words are not mine either. And *your* Aeneas is no great stormfowl. But you need one. *How* you need one. A great stormfowl, an arch-especial spirit, to land beside you and drag your story to the greatness of mine.'

The train jolted along the tunnel under the Thames. I could sense the weight of water above. The windows misted up as if the water were reaching through the earth to get at us.

'Why do you keep talking about stormfowls?'

'Because that is what someone, not me, not you, will write.'

'*Will* write?'

For answer he too looked at the misty windows. 'You were brought to the train by a guide. What did he say as he left you?'

I thought back. ' "A safe journey and an informative one",' I replied.

He still peered through the windows as he spoke. 'In this place, we are outside time, you and I.'

I didn't understand this. 'I have to be *in* time,'

I said. 'I get off at Waterloo. I'm going to the Purcell Room. I mustn't be late.'

'The Purcell Room? So he has a room of his own, does he? Will you see him there?'

The train drew in to Waterloo. The doors opened.

'You have arrived, safe and informed,' said the man. 'Remember me. And look for your stormfowl.'

The doors closed. I saw the silver train, empty still except for his shadowy form, draw out. I watched it take the right-hand tunnel immediately at the end of the platform and disappear.

Then I remembered the Northern Line map. There *was* no right-hand tunnel at the south end of Waterloo tube station. I could see the single track stretch shining and unbroken into the darkness ahead.

Mystified, I turned. The message on the dot-matrix indicator was changing: 2ND TRAIN: KENNINGTON 2 MINS at the bottom disappeared; NEXT TRAIN: KENNINGTON formed at the top. But I just caught part of the original message at the top as it faded as if at the crowing of the cock. —ADES.

I could remember no station on the Northern Line south of Waterloo which ended in —ADES.

As I stood trying to work all this out, the packed Kennington train arrived, silver, with UNDERGROUND written in red on the side. Now came another thought. Did my train have UNDER-

GROUND painted in red on the side? Or was it UNDERWORLD?

I shook my head as if to clear the fog that seemed to cloud my brain. Who had I travelled with? Who first wrote down the story of Dido and Aeneas? Who had guided the great poet Dante through the Underworld? Surely I had not been in the company of . . . ? I was all at once creased with shame about some of the lunatic things I had just said to . . . I couldn't bear to think of what had just passed between me and . . . VIRGIL?

Yes, my journey had been both safe *and* informative, but I stood there a sadder and a wiser man. It was time to leave this half-world and seek the upper air. I turned – to see my guide beside me on the platform at Waterloo.

Up the escalator, up the steps, up a narrow, dark spiral staircase echoing with the same cries and moans I had heard on my first journey. Into a cavernous, rocky chamber, dank, dripping and cold, where the echoes deafened and turned into shrieks of damned and tormented souls in circles far away. Thence to a crack of light where two mighty rocks joined only to part as my guide extended that same gaunt arm – then a scramble through screening bushes and finally in intoxicating fresh air and bright, warm sunshine, into the flat meadows with nothing before me but the wide river, across which I could see the gleaming white dome of the still-new St Paul's cathedral.

Yes, here I was in the sunshine, still only half knowing who I was.

'Master Tate.'

My first guide again. But dressed differently: knee breeches, long coat, wig. As was I.

'Master Tate,' he repeated. 'What are you doing here? Tonight of all nights. You are on the wrong side of the river. Why, is it not tonight that they perform your new operatic piece at Mr Priest's establishment in Chelsea? *Dido and Aeneas*, for which Master Purcell has written the music?'

Yes, of course. I, Nahum Tate, the hack writer with delusions of grandeur, and Henry Purcell, the young and promising composer, had acceded to the request of our friend Josias Priest and together written the piece for the young ladies of his academy.

'You are right. How foolish of me to be decanted here in the wrong place.'

'Hire a skiff to take you across the Thames,' said my one-time guide. 'You'll be in time.'

The boatman rowed; the water rippled. I looked back at the receding bank and sought the rock portal through which I had emerged. I saw only meadows to the water's edge. My guide had disappeared. Back to the Underworld from whence he had come? I turned to the ferryman and it crossed my mind to ask his name and what river it was that he bore me over. But before I could frame the question, my memory seemed to fade; my recent encounter blurred and dissolved. I shook my head: for the moment, all that was gone. It was replaced by a delighted anticipation of what I was soon to see and hear. Cool strings, tinkling harpsichord continuo, soaring voices making air of angels from my lumbering words – 'Remember me, but ah! forget my fate.' And then I knew that in very truth the great stormfowl had landed on my shore.

TEARS OF A CLOWN

Geraldine McCaughrean

Based on the opera
I PAGLIACI (THE STROLLING PLAYERS)
Composer and librettist: Ruggiero Leoncavallo (1858–1919)
First performed: Milan 1892

'Same old story,' said the Judge when his son pressed him to talk about the trial. Though it had caused a great stir in the district, it represented nothing remarkable to the old man. He had presided over similar trials many, many times. 'Jealous husband, pretty young wife. Actors, of course – well, hardly better than gypsies, really. No discipline, you know. Can't keep a grip of themselves. Seen it all before. Same old story.'

The first thing the villagers heard was a thud-thud like a heartbeat. Then a jangle of music – a ribald trumpet, a quacking cornet – heralded the arrival of the players.

'The actors are coming! The harlequins! Canio's Company! They're back!'

'Do you remember last year?'

'Remember? I laughed so hard I fell off the bench!'

'Those songs. Couldn't get them out of my mind for a week.'

'My wife hasn't stopped talking about it yet.'

'Did you see the plays, Silvio? Remember that pretty girl who played Columbine? What was she called? Canio's wife, lucky old devil. What *was* she called?'

'Nedda.'

'Ah yes. Nedda. I'll be glad to see her again!'

Oh yes, Silvio remembered. He remembered purple summer nights full of stars and crickets and the smell of scythed grass. He remembered Nedda: once seen never forgotten. Pretty Nedda: once kissed never forgettable. The young man laid down his spade and watched the strolling players rattle into the village square: a rickety donkey cart, a bucketful of cheap props, a hamperful of spangled costumes. The people round about were delighted at the prospect of a break in Life's dull routine: a saucy pantomime, a knockabout comedy. But the thrill in Silvio's heart was far greater. The joy coming his way was flesh and blood. Real.

There were only four actors in the troupe: three men and a woman. There was Canio, the playmaster (who played Mr Punch – 'Pagliaccio'); his wife Nedda (who played Columbine); a hunchback clown called Tonio whose deformity got laughs all by itself. And there was Peppé: fetcher, carrier, fixer and mender – whether of props, costumes or quarrels.

What did it matter if the show did not change much from one year's end to the next? Its audiences loved it just *because* they knew it so well – the jokes, the slapstick, the sentimental tear-jerking, the happy ending. The cart drew to a halt. Nedda – a woman who carried her beauty about like a winner's trophy – bunched her skirts together to climb down. The calf she bared had the bloom of a peach.

From the tailgate of the cart, the hunchback rushed forward to help her down. But all he got for his pains was a shove that sent him sprawling. 'Keep your hands to yourself, Tonio,' said Canio spitefully. 'My wife's perfectly capable of getting off a cart.'

The crowd loved it, of course. They were in the mood to laugh. When a comic opens his mouth, everyone looks for a joke to come out. They jeered and hissed Tonio as they would do in the theatre. Besides, Tonio was built like a fairy tale troll – someone Nature intended for a kick and a punch and a gale of laughter to blow him away.

'Welcome back, Canio! Come for a drink! Glad to see you again, old man! Come for a pint or three!'

Canio was quick to take up the offer. (Peppé was even quicker and he had not even been asked.)

'Are you coming, Tonio?'

'Someone's got to see to the donkey,' replied the hunchback sullenly.

Some wit remarked, over-loud, ''Spect he wants to be alone with Nedda, eh? Eh?' The crowd began to laugh uproariously. But then something in the playmaster's face – a quick, livid colouring of the broken veins in his cheeks – choked their laughter.

'Ah, now there's the difference between theatre and real life, you see,' he said with a grimace masquerading as a smile. 'In *Harlequin and Columbine*, in come I – Pagliaccio – and find my wife and her lover canoodling. And what happens? All that happens is that Harlequin gets his ears boxed. Or I do . . . But just you see what'd happen in real life, if I found my wife with a lover. There'd be a different ending to that play, I can tell you.'

A sudden gust of wind shook the poplars into a trembling hiss and Nedda pulled her shawl round her and uttered a little cry, as if the cold had caught her unawares. The onlookers shuffled their feet, rather embarrassed by Canio's outburst. He saw their unease. 'But that's just why I'm the luckiest man alive!' he cried cheerily, sweeping both hands into the air. 'Because my Nedda never gives me a moment's sadness! My Nedda only ever brings me joy! That's why I adore her. Here! Give me a kiss, my adorable little Columbine, then let's us men all go and drink a toast to True Love!' The villagers cheered and swept him away, on a raft of goodwill, to the inn. Canio was, after all, a clown. He knew how to work an audience.

Darkness fell so softly that day that the sound of the church bell ringing for evening prayers seemed like the sound of dusk tumbling to earth. The starlings and bats flitting between the rooftops could almost have been the visible notes of music written on the purpling air. Long after everyone else had wandered out of the square, either to church or to the inn, Nedda stood mesmerized by the sights and sound of sunset. She was still trembling. 'What did he mean by that? "If I found my wife with a lover"? Does he suspect, then? Does he? Does he know about me and Silvio? Never! He'd never have brought the Company back here if he did. Back to Silvio's village. Oh, Silvio!'

It was a name she had carried with her for a year, like a lucky charm hidden out of sight. Silvio. It was a half-remembered face; a sunny recollection of the previous summer; a lovely idea grown to perfection inside her head. 'Oh, Silvio! I wish I were as free as these birds to fly to you whenever you called my name—'

'Nedda!'

She caught her breath, then said in disappointed disgust, 'Oh. It's you, is it?' Tonio should have stayed in the shadows. In the open she could see him for the gargoyle he was. 'Why aren't you in the inn with the rest?'

'I couldn't tear myself away from the sight of you. My eyes wouldn't let me,' said Tonio.

Nedda snorted with exasperation. 'Have you any idea how ridiculous you sound saying things like that?'

'Why? Is love only for the lovely, then?' said Tonio, limping closer. 'Can I help it if it's your face I see in my dreams? Can I help it if I burn with love at the very sight of you? I am a man, after all.'

'A *man*? Is that what you call it? Blagh! If I saw you lying in the street, I wouldn't tread on you: that's what you are.'

'Well, you heartless little—'

'Don't come any closer.'

With the pleading gone from his voice, Tonio was more frightening. 'Not a man, eh? I'll show you how much of a man I am—'

'Keep away! Keep off, you – you *object*!' Nedda snatched up the whip from the driving seat of the cart and struck out with it, slashing Tonio across the face. All the birds in the village square took flight at the noise.

Tonio recoiled like a gun. One moment he was treading on her skirt hem, the next he was scuttling away into the shadows. Treat a man like an animal and bitterness can soon transform him into part-beast. 'I'll get even for that!' bellowed the beast out of the darkness. *'I'll make you pay!'*

'What was all that about?' asked Silvio, leaping over a high stone wall. Just when Nedda needed him most, there he stood beside her, his arm circling her waist, his eyes bright with starlight. A year's separation had changed nothing.

'Oh, just one more misery in a world of miseries!' she cried melodramatically and burst into self-pitying tears, clinging tightly to him. 'I hate my life! I hate my fate! I hate the theatre and the never-ending travelling. I hate the people I have to be with. I hate having to be apart from you!'

'Well, there's an easy answer to that, isn't there?' whispered Silvio soothingly. 'Come away with me. Now. Tonight. I asked you a year ago but you didn't have the courage to break away. Do it now. I dare you. Leave Canio. Leave the theatre. Finish with this appalling life of yours and run away with me. We'll live happily ever after.'

'Like in the fairy stories.'

'Our life will be one long fairy story.'

'But I'm a married woman, Silvio! My husband . . .'

She argued and he persuaded. She threw up obstacles and he knocked them down. The joy was in standing together, breast and breast, imagining how different life could be in a perfect world. They were so absorbed that neither saw Tonio, walking off his anger in the sweet evening air. He saw them, but said nothing – simply slipped away in the direction of the inn.

'I don't know,' whimpered Nedda. 'It would break Canio's heart if I left him.'

'Canio? He's a clown. He'll laugh it off. The theatre's more important to him than you are.'

'You're right,' she said doubtfully, and then, *'You're right!* Meet me tonight, after the play!' They kissed, then Silvio, showing off, left the way he had come, springing over the wall.

'Until tonight, then! I'm yours tonight and for ever!' she called after him.

If Tonio had written the scene himself, he

could not have wished for better timing. Arm-in-arm with Canio, steering him into the village square, Tonio fetched the playmaster just in time to hear Nedda call out, *'I'm yours tonight and for ever!'* It was the sweetest revenge a spurned lover could possibly hope for.

When he heard Nedda call, some portion of Canio's brain burst, spilling acid or boiling lead through every thought, with a searing, molten desolation. Glimpsing only a shirt and a tuft of hair vaulting away into darkness, he broke from Tonio and ran at the wall as if he would smash his way through it. He bloodied his hands trying to pull himself up. Below him Nedda hung on his belt to hinder him, but he shook her off and tumbled clumsily over the coping-stones.

Aghast, her mouth gaping, Nedda turned to see Tonio gloating triumphantly, sniggering and snickering like a grinning idiot.

'Happy now?' she asked, and the ice in her voice scored Tonio like a dagger.

A dagger.

When Canio came back, he was holding a dagger. In the darkness he had soon lost track of Silvio's fleeing shadow and did not waste time searching for him. Instead, he went back to his wife, armed with a knife, to demand the name of her illicit lover.

'Don't be a fool, Canio!' exclaimed Peppé, chancing along at a moment of terrifying menace. 'Put the knife away, Canio! Put it down.'

'Not till she tells me who she just arranged to sleep with tonight!' screamed Canio.

'Never. I won't tell you a thing,' was all Nedda would say.

She said it so coolly, with such shameless defiance, that anything might have happened if Peppé had not leapt in and forced Canio's white fingers from round the knife's hilt. 'Control yourself, man! What are you thinking of? Church is nearly over! People will be coming over this way to the theatre! They want a play, old friend. They want *Harlequin and Columbine*. They want a comedy, man. You aren't going to give them a tragedy instead, are you?'

But Canio was deaf to gentle, conciliatory Peppé. The only words he heard were Tonio's, whispered in his ear like the Devil's own advice. 'Leave it. Leave it for now, Canio. You'll get your chance later,' said the hunchback. 'Loverboy's bound to come and see his ladyfriend on stage, isn't he? He'll be in the audience tonight, you take my word. You'll pick him out easy. He'll give himself away. Later, later.'

'Later,' said Canio.

'That's right. Later. Come on, old chap,' said Peppé, slapping him heartily on the shoulder. 'Get your costume on for the play. You'll feel different once you've got your costume on. You know what they say: the play must go on!'

With a *crack, crack, crack* which Canio took for his skull splitting, the hunchback began to beat on a drum – beating up an audience, announcing the imminent start of the evening's entertainment. *Crack. Crack. Crack.* Like a heartbeat. Or like a heart breaking in pieces.

Canio opened the door of the little dressing room behind the village stage. His costume, hanging up behind the door, jerked like some practical joker jumping out at him: *Boo!* Baggy pants. Baggy sleeves. An absurd hat with scrubby feathers. Canio threw himself down in the chair and stared at his reflection in the mirror: a small, old mirror speckled as if by some blight. His face blighted. His life blighted.

He scragged back his lank, dishevelled hair and daubed his face with greasepaint – larded his features as if they so revolted him that he wanted to paint them out. Two whorls of white round his eyes; two new eyebrows raised in permanent astonishment; huge black lashes like spiders crouched over his eyesockets; cherry-red cheeks garish against the deathly white of the lardy greasepaint. He annihilated his own features until the face in the mirror was the face of a stranger gaping back at him: a gormless mooncalf, a grinning fool. He obliterated the grey wound of his true mouth with a grotesque upward curve of scarlet – a whore's mouth, a clown's mouth, a mouth eternally laughing.

Out of the mirror the mouth said to him,

'That's it, Pagliaccio. Go on. Daub it on thick. The paint, the powder. Dress up in the baggy clothes. Your public's waiting for you, aren't they? They want their laughs. They need their entertainment . . . What's that? Your wife's cuckolded you? Your heart's cracked its bell? Your guts are scalding with misery? Is that what the public pay for? Is that what they want to hear? Laugh, Mr Punch – Signor Pagliaccio! Laugh!

'What's that? There's a pain in you like a rat gnawing on your brain? That's not very funny, Punchinello. You'll have to do better than that. This is theatre! Didn't you know? Columbine and Harlequin have been lovers for a hundred years or more! It's only a bit of fun. A kiss here. A romp there. Pagliaccio's one big laugh! Silly old cuckold. Oh *come* now, Mr Punch. Not *tears*! Your make-up will run. You'll spoil that face of yours.'

With a cry of a man tormented, Canio threw the mirror to the floor and the glass broke with a loud crack, just as a bell rang to signal the start of the play.

The benches in front of the theatre are full. Nedda has been round with a collection plate. The takings are good tonight. She is already wearing her pretty spangled costume. But of course she doesn't actually *become* Columbine until she steps up on to the stage and the play begins. She sings that her old husband Pagliaccio will be home late. Why so anxious, then, about the evening's supper? The servant has not brought it yet. Then, from behind the scenes, comes the voice of her faithful Harlequin singing a serenade. A sentimental sigh runs round the audience. Lips smile fondly at the prospect of a familiar happiness.

'At last, Taddeo! Where have you been, you good-for-nothing servant! Have you brought the chicken for our supper?'

The upward glare of the guttering, oil footlights cast remarkably unpleasant shadows on Tonio's face tonight. As the lazy servant declares his ardent love for Columbine and she flounces about the room preparing supper, ignoring him entirely, the audience hold their sides laughing. But the shadows flicker even so, making a rubbery mask out of Tonio's face.

Ah! Over the windowsill leaps Harlequin, for a supper of chicken and kisses. *'Aaaah!'* sigh the crowd, and the gruesome servant is dismissed with the sole of a boot. Oho! Here's a sleeping draught for that old buffoon Pagliaccio! So the night ahead promises nothing but bliss for the two lovers.

But partway through supper, in bursts that ugly servant again – to say that Pagliaccio has *come home early*!!

Quick, Harlequin! Out of the window! The crowd rises involuntarily on their haunches, willing the boy in the diamond-chequered suit to get away safely. His lovely Columbine calls after him:

'Until tonight, then! I'm yours tonight and for ever!'

'I'm yours tonight and for ever!' All evening those words had been echoing in Canio's head. Hearing them now, as he waited in the wings, a mist descended on him which blurred all distinction between Drama and real life, between madness and sanity.

Oh, he spoke the right lines when he entered: 'Who's been here? You've had some lover here with you, I know! Who is he? What's his name?' But there was such venom in the way he spoke them!

'What's his name?'

The script was going awry. That line should have been . . .

'Tell me his name!'

'Oh come now, Pagliaccio . . .' said Columbine.

Not any more! No! Not Pagliaccio any more! Not me! Pagliaccio's dead. A man needs his honour, you see? He can't live without his honour, no more than breathe underwater. Can't live, you see? Not without revenge. It's my fault, I admit it! I should never have given my love to a woman like you. I should have found someone who deserved it – who'd respect it. Give it back to me!'

Nedda improvised desperately. 'Well, if I'm so unworthy, husband, set me free – whistle me off – send me away.' She tried to make the lines sound light and spirited, her voice swooping up and down with exaggerated jollity. It only served to taunt Canio into an apoplectic rage.

'Not till I know the name of your lover!'

'Ah ha ha ha ha! What a jealous old fool you are to make such a tragedy out of a bit of fun!' trilled Nedda, moving about the stage faster and faster, her broad skirts extinguishing footlights as she tried to keep her distance from Canio.

The audience stirred restlessly, glanced sideways at one another. A strange variation this, on the old traditional play? Some laughed nervously. Silvio had risen to his feet without realizing it. The harlequin Peppé went to place himself between man and wife, to keep anything worse from happening. But he found the hunchback was holding him by both wrists, grinning that snarling grin of his. A phenomenally strong man, Tonio. Peppé could not break free.

'His name, or I'll kill you,' shouted Canio, sweat and tears crazing his face with rivulets of black and red.

'Look out, he's got a knife!' Amid panic, a bench in the audience overturned. As he ran forward to the stage, his own dagger drawn, Silvio stumbled over the bench.

So he was too late to stop Canio from plunging the knife into Nedda's chest.

A redness decorated her pretty dress, blinded

the spangles one by one. Her mouth, painted for the stage into a small crimson bow, showed no expression. 'Silvio!' she said, seeing her lover's face loom over her husband's shoulder. Then she died.

Canio whirled round and stuck out his blade so that Silvio virtually ran on to it: his heart impaled on Canio's knife. He was dead before his face hit the floor.

A great stillness had fallen over the theatre. The audience stared. Pagliaccio stared back. Peppé, powerless to undo what had been done, stood limp as a harlequin puppet. The hunchback had let him go now, his ugly hands covering his ugly face in horror.

Drawing one baggy sleeve across his face, Pagliaccio wiped away his greasepaint features and Canio's face emerged from beneath, an ageing, grieving man bereft of the women he had loved year upon loveless year.

The audience stared, Canio stared back. What were they waiting for? The rest of the play? Their money's worth? 'You can go home now,' he said. 'The comedy's over.'

'Seen it all before. Same old story,' said the Judge, recounting the trial to his son.

'But that wasn't a story,' said his son. 'It was real life. This really happened.'

The old man showed his irritability with a puckering of lips as dry and tissuey as the court documents he was filing away. 'Some of these people can't tell the difference. Between the nonsense they act on stage and the foolishness they get up to off-stage. You don't want to go feeling sorry for that kind. No self-discipline, you see . . . My courtroom was packed to the doors every day, of course. People always seem to find murder trials entertaining.'

'I wish I had been there,' said his son.

'Whatever for? No great legal event. Only some actor killing some actress. Only the same old story.'

THE THREEPENNY
OPERA

Jon Blake

Based on Brecht and Weill's
THE THREEPENNY OPERA, after
THE BEGGAR'S OPERA
Composer: Original arrangements by John Pepusch
Librettist: John Gay (1685–1732)
First performed: London 1728

I was there the day MacHeath went to his death. *THIS EVIL MAN*, said the *Mirror*. *MACHEATH EXECUTION TO GO AHEAD AS APPEAL FAILS*, said the *Guardian*. *DIE YOU BASTARD*, said the *Sun*.

There had been a big debate as to how it should be done. Hanging was too old-fashioned. The electric chair was too expensive. The gas chamber reminded people of Hitler. In the end they settled on a lethal injection, administered by a qualified doctor.

Satellite TV got the broadcast rights. They set up a giant video screen at Tyburn. An eerie silence fell as the doctor searched for a vein. Then . . . well, I'd better tell the whole story.

My name? Damien Filch. Came to London at fifteen? Why? Parents. They wouldn't let me have my own life. They were in my face night and day. They left me with no choice.

I never felt anything when the door slammed behind me. I just walked to the station and got on the first train. I had friends in London, and I was sure they would put me up. I never even thought to ring them. Then we pulled into Paddington, and suddenly this terrible feeling of loneliness came over me. I wasn't as big as I thought. I ran to the phone, stabbed out the number, and got a long, sinister monotone. Disconnected.

I was homeless.

I went to a policeman and asked if he knew any hostels. He advised me to take the next train home. I rang the Sally Army. They had nothing. I went up to strangers, more desperate each time, but no one could help.

Next day, after a sleepless night, I was begging.

I was sure I'd soon get out of it. I told myself things could only get better. Then these two guys came up to me. 'You got a licence?' they said. 'What, a licence to beg?' I said. 'We call it street trading,' they said. 'Piss off,' I said. They laid into me. They really gave me a kicking. Then they handed me a business card:

PEACHUM PROMOTIONS.

'Next time, you ring us first,' they said.

Next day, I visited this outfit. I sat in a tacky office, with plywood walls and dying pot-plants. In came a fat guy in a suit, looked like an over-grown school bully. I started to give him my story and he started to check his Rolex.

'You the one we picked up by Paddington?' he said, not even looking at me.

'Yeah, do you want to see the bruises?' I said.

'Good,' he said. 'The boys did their job.'

The guy told me to call him Mr Peachum. He sniffed my breath for drink. Then he showed me a map of London, squared off into numbered districts. You couldn't beg in those districts without a licence from him. It was all in our interests, mind. Stopped us fighting each other. Besides, people were hardened to homeless people. We needed professional marketing. All it would cost was five quid down and fifty per cent of my take.

I signed. Peachum gave me the official P P collection box, a badge, and a cardboard cap. I was admiring my new look when in came Mrs Peachum.

'Where's Polly?' said Peachum. He talked to his wife like she was a servant.

'Upstairs, I 'spect,' said Mrs P, who looked like she didn't much care about anything.

'I don't want her seeing that fellow,' said Peachum. 'She's too young. Too easily taken in. Next thing we know she'll be married. Blabbing all the company secrets.'

'Seems quite a nice man,' said Mrs P, with a shrug.

Peachum closed his wife into a corner. His voiced dropped. 'You've met him?'

Mrs P nodded. 'They say he was an officer,' she said. 'Oo, and he does dress *beautifully*.'

Peachum's eyes narrowed. 'White kid gloves?' he asked.

'How did you know?' asked Mrs P.

Peachum stormed from the room. His footsteps thudded up the stairs. A door slammed. The footsteps thudded down, faster. Peachum crashed into the room, eyes bulging.

'She's not there!' he cried. 'And her bed hasn't been slept in!'

'Oh,' said Mrs P. 'Maybe she's with a friend.'

'Let's pray she is,' snapped Peachum, 'because the man you described . . . that man is Mac the Knife.'

After a few days I gave up hope of finding a place in a hostel. I built myself a den in Lincolns Inn Fields, out of wooden pallets and polythene. I made friends with the people round about – a few nutters, mainly nice, ordinary people. Our little shanty town stood smack in the middle of the Inns of Court. That's where the lawyers go, in their Mercs and their Jags, running the great British justice system.

I had one possession – a Walkman. When I wasn't on the scrounge, I found myself somewhere warm and comfortable and listened to U2, or some other multi-millionaire pop stars. I was soon kicked out of all the libraries, the galleries and the burger bars. I started on the furniture shops, especially the ones with big, plush, high-backed armchairs. Not that I was mad about big, plush, high-backed armchairs – it was just more difficult for the shop assistants to see you in them.

Anyway, one day I found myself in a real luxury store. The prices on the tickets were jokes. It was like someone had thought up a number and doubled it. I curled up in an armchair, stinking of fresh leather, and warmed my batteries in my hand to get a bit more life out of them.

That was when I saw him. He swanned into the store like he owned it. He was so impeccable, he didn't seem real. You just knew his suit was Armani and his shoes were Gucci. But what really caught my attention was the white kid gloves.

I pushed the batteries into the Walkman and switched on Record. My fingers were like fumbling sausages. The man they called Mac the Knife gave a nod, and in walked Polly.

I knew it was Polly straight away. She was sixteen going on twenty-five. She was dressed to the nines but looked like a fish out of water. I decided it was my mission to save her from this man.

'We'll take this,' said MacHeath, touching an obscenely expensive dining table.

'We shouldn't buy mahogany,' said Polly. 'Because of the rainforests.'

MacHeath chuckled. He put a finger under Polly's chin and drew her towards him. 'It's rosewood,' he whispered.

I was ready to throw up. He was treating her like a five-year-old. She didn't have the confidence to resist.

'May I offer you our catalogue, sir?' asked a salesman.

MacHeath brushed the catalogue aside. He'd already made up his mind. His white-gloved finger picked out the goodies like a blackbird picking worms. When I realized what he was spending, it made me catch my breath.

'Do you have an account, sir?' asked the salesman.

MacHeath flashed a gold credit card. The salesman dashed to the till and Polly squeezed Mac's arm. Moments later the deal was done.

'Thank you very much, Mr Farquhar,' said the salesman, checking the name on the gold credit card.

It wasn't long before I came across Polly again. Next day, in fact. She breezed into Peachum's with a pair of leather suitcases and announced she was leaving.

'Oh no you're not!' cried Peachum.

Polly put down the suitcases and looked her father in the eyes. Mac had programmed her for this.

'Well you may as well know,' she said. 'I'm married.'

Peachum hit the roof. 'You stupid, stupid

girl!' he railed. 'He's a bloody murderer! A thief! A rapist!'

'None of that was proven,' said Polly.

'Yes, and we know why,' said Peachum.

I didn't know why, but I had a feeling I'd better not ask.

'Why didn't you tell us you were getting married?' asked Mrs P, gently. It was like the hard-cop-soft-cop routine.

'Why?' said Polly. 'This is why!'

To my disbelief, Polly turned straight to me. 'Can you help me with these?' she said, offering her suitcases.

Mrs P's jaw dropped. 'Polly!' she gasped. Talking to the down-and-outs was a big taboo, which is no doubt why Polly did it. But she was half joking. She gave me a wink and vanished upstairs.

Peachum sank into his chair with his head in his hands. 'Who's going to answer the phone?' he moaned. 'Who's going to keep the Old Bill sweet?'

Mrs P glanced at the morning paper. *DEATH PENALTY RETURNS* was the headline. 'There must be a way to get him,' she murmured.

I felt the cassette in my pocket. A week ago I would have backed off, not got involved. Now I snapped at the chance. ''Scuse me,' I said. 'Got something you might be interested in.'

I reported what I'd seen in the furniture store. I showed Peachum the cassette, the perfect evidence.

His lizard eyes lit up. A hand reached for the cassette.

'What's it worth?' I asked, snatching it away.

'Huh!' sniffed Peachum. 'A hustler now, are you?'

'No choice, Mr Peachum,' I said. Beneath my super-cool act, my heart was thudding like a piston.

'Let's hear it first,' said Peachum.

I shook his clammy hand and handed him the tape. I was in the game now, a dealer. Peachum took the tape into the back room, while Mrs P shot me a suspicious glance, followed by a token smile. From the back room I heard the mumbly tones of Mac the Knife offering the stolen credit card. Peachum came back, looking satisfied.

'How much?' I gabbled. I'd made up my mind to ask a grand, but accept anything over fifty quid.

'You can keep it,' said Peachum, handing back the tape.

I was gobsmacked. 'You don't want it?' I gasped.

Peachum held up a second tape. 'Terrible thing, piracy,' he mused.

What could I do? I was powerless as ever.

I started stealing soon after that. Just small things. I took a Biro, then a pork pie, then a car blanket. It gave me a high. Why not, I thought to myself. No one cares if I'm alive or dead. Well then, I'll act like I'm dead, and nothing matters.

Nothing mattered to Mac the Knife, that was for sure. They arrested him in a massage parlour. Three days after he'd married Polly, he was back to his old habits. That's how he started off, pimping. Word was that Mrs P bribed one of his old girls to turn him in. There's just no honour anywhere.

Polly couldn't understand it. Mac had told her he'd gone to a business meeting. Mind you, that could have been true. Where better to chat up a few bent politicians?

How do I know all this? Because Polly told me. At first I think she spoke to me because it was forbidden. Then she realized I was sympathetic, not out to use her like everyone else. She liked my sense of humour, and the fact I could take the piss out of myself. I liked the fact that, despite everything, she still had a sense of right and wrong.

But Mac still impressed her. Soon as she found out where he was held, she decided to visit, with me for company. Believe me, I was nervous. Walking round the East End with Mac the Knife's wife was not my idea of safety. Then, when we reached the prison, she insisted I came down to Mac's cell.

'I'm sure he'll like you,' she said.

Yes, I thought to myself. Especially if he recognizes me from the furniture store.

There was a surprise in store for both of us. Mac already had a visitor. A woman. A young woman. An attractive young woman.

Polly stopped in her tracks. The woman looked her up and down. 'Hello, Polly,' she said.

Polly composed herself again, and walked up to the cell. Mac was lounging back against the wall, inspecting his nails. He wasn't at all put out by the situation. 'Hiya, darling,' he said.

'Are you going to introduce us?' said Polly.

'This is Lucy,' replied Mac. 'She's doing me a favour.'

'Be seeing you, Mac,' said Lucy. She brushed past Polly and left.

Polly's face was like stone. She'd convinced herself Mac had good reason to be in the massage parlour. Now she was having doubts.

'You better see the boys,' said Mac. 'Make sure they're looking after the accounts.'

'I can look after the accounts,' said Polly.

Mac just smiled.

'I used to look after Dad's,' added Polly.

'Honey,' said Mac, 'we're talking about a lot of money. Not a post office book.'

At this point, Mac caught sight of me. For the first time, I was eye-to-eye with the big cheese, the gang boss, the cold-blooded killer. This, maybe, was my future.

'Hi,' I said.

Mac looked at Polly, then back at me. His eyes narrowed.

'We're just friends,' I added.

With one eye on me, Mac reached through the bars, took Polly's chin in his hand, and kissed her. 'I'll be seeing you soon, darling,' he said, softly.

'How come?' asked Polly.

Mac put a finger on Polly's lips. 'Everything's in hand,' he whispered.

Later that night we heard that Mac the Knife was free.

Peachum ripped the newspaper in two. 'What crap!' he railed. 'MacHeath never escaped! They let him out, the bastards!'

I sensed another chance to get in with Peachum.

'There was a woman with him,' I said. 'Maybe she had something to do with it.'

Peachum swallowed his fourth Rennie and turned to me. 'What did she look like?' he snapped.

'Red hair . . . about five-five . . . oh, and her name was Lucy.'

'Lucy Brown,' said Peachum. 'I thought so. Daughter of the great Chief Inspector.' He turned to Mrs P. 'Didn't I tell you? They're as thick as thieves, Brownie and MacHeath. Old army buddies.'

So that was why Mac had got away with so much! I should have guessed. The system stank from top to bottom.

A wave of something like sympathy crossed Mrs P's face. 'Poor Polly,' she said.

'Never mind her!' railed Peachum. 'What about us? Mac's sure to know we got him arrested. He'll kill us!'

The full weight of the situation sank in. Mr

and Mrs P sat silent and grim, planning their next move. Behind them, the radio news chattered on. London was preparing for its biggest event for a decade – the G7 Summit. The seven most powerful men in the world were coming to town. Peachum was unimpressed.

'Not going to save me, are they?' he muttered.

On that happy note, I took leave of Peachum Promotions, and retired to my humble den. I found two of the pallets smashed to pieces and polythene scattered all over the place.

'What's gone on?' I asked Greg, my neighbour.

'We've just had the law in,' replied Greg, who was piecing together his tent poles.

'Why?' I gasped.

'They're combing the area,' said Greg. 'Looking for bombs.'

'*Here?*'

'Everywhere.'

'They never had to smash up our homes!'

'We were lucky, mate. Those down on the river have been cleaned out altogether.'

'Why?'

'You tell me, mate. They were in the way of the cameras, that's my opinion.'

Sick at heart, I began to patch together my den. That was when I made an awful discovery. My Walkman was missing.

'Frankie had it,' said Greg. 'He's gone.'

Of all the things that had happened, this hit me the worst. I'd shared a ham roll with Frankie the night before. I laid down, pulled a blanket over my head, and cried.

I don't think I slept at all that night. I thrashed around in anger and frustration, thinking of bombs, and guns, and violent protests. My mind kept going down to the river, where the cameras would be. I thought of killing myself, dramatically. I thought of killing the Prime Minister. Then I began to wonder about the homeless people, where they'd gone, what they were doing. Bit by bit, a plan formed in my mind. It was a plan which would fix MacHeath for good, and his crooked pals in the police. It was a plan which would get that parasite Peachum off our backs, wreck the Summit, and shock the world into action. All I had to do was set it in motion.

I rose with the sun. I breakfasted on the lawyer's cold chips. Then I paced around the Fields, psyching myself up, rehearsing my words to Peachum. I was no longer a thief. I was an activist.

Ten past nine, I sat in the office of Peachum Promotions. Workmen were busy fitting alarms and security devices. Peachum skulked in like a cornered rat, a baseball bat in his hand. When he saw me, he turned on his secretary.

'I told you!' he rasped. 'No unauthorized personnel!'

The secretary cowered. I jumped to my feet. 'Mr Peachum,' I said, 'I've got a proposal.'

'What for?' snapped Peachum, moving menacingly towards me.

'To save you, for a start,' I said.

Peachum reached for the door handle. Then he stopped. Maybe he remembered the tape I'd made before. Maybe he realized I wasn't totally stupid.

'Make it quick,' he said.

I was like a dog shown its lead. 'The Summit starts in two days,' I said. 'They're going walkabout down by the river. Don't ask me how I know, I just do. It's a photo-opportunity. They want a nice shot in front of Big Ben. But I know how to wreck it.'

Peachum's brow furrowed. 'How?' he snapped.

'Get the homeless down there. All of them.'

Peachum was dubious. 'How does that save me?' he said.

'Easy. Brownie is sure to be in charge of security. His neck will be on the line if anything goes wrong. So we give him an ultimatum. Get MacHeath back behind bars, or else.'

Peachum was still not convinced. 'You'll never get those down-and-outs off their arses,' he said. 'It's hard enough to get six of them down this office.'

I smiled. 'That's 'cos they're paying *you*,' I

said. 'If you were paying *them*, it would be a different matter.'

Peachum was aghast. 'Me, pay them!?'

My heart began to thump. 'Yeah, all the money you've extorted from us, you bastard!'

Peachum's hand seized hard on the handle of the baseball bat. I held my ground.

'You've got no choice, Peachum!' I said. Then I turned slowly and walked towards the door, bracing myself for the splintering pain which could happen at any second. It never came.

The word spread like bushfire. Every person had to tell ten people, then each of those told ten more. At first we reckoned on a thousand, then ten thousand, then a hundred thousand. When you realized the numbers involved, you realized the kind of profit Peachum had been making. That plywood office was just for show.

Meanwhile Peachum delivered the ultimatum to Brownie. Brownie knew we meant business. The coppers saw us gathering in gangs. They read the placards we made from the cardboard we slept under. They tried putting on the pressure. A few people got mysteriously beaten up. A hostel got fire-bombed by fascists. Rumours started, including one that I was a state agent. The whole city seemed to be turning paranoid. It was a test of nerve.

But it was Brownie's nerve that cracked. The

day before the Summit, Mac the Knife was rearrested, in Lucy Brown's flat. He was tried in a no-jury Diplock Court, like the ones in Northern Ireland. Then, to everyone's amazement, he was sentenced to death.

It was obvious why they'd done it. If MacHeath stayed alive, the truth would come out about his friendship with the Chief Inspector. Who knows what other corruption was hidden? These kind of things went right to the top. They were built into the system.

But if they were hoping we would call off the demo, they had another think coming. We had no such intention. That evening, we stood outside Rumbelows' window, watching the world leaders arrive at Heathrow. We saw the handshakes, the backslaps, and the way they laughed at each other's little jokes. Tomorrow we would wipe the smiles right off their faces.

The scene next morning was unforgettable. At first it was dribs and drabs, but as we approached the river, it was obvious the turnout was huge. Some came with placards, some with their blankets, but all with a sense of purpose. It was like something out of the Middle Ages, like the victims of some great plague. But it was not nature that had made us like this.

The police operation was surprisingly low-key. I expected to see side-streets packed with armoured vans. I expected to see horses, riot gear, whole areas cordoned off. All we saw were a few officers keeping a weather eye on us.

Something was wrong.

We reached the embankment. There were homeless people as far as the eye could see. But there were no other crowds, no cameras, and no Peachum. For half an hour we waited. Then an hour. The crowd became increasingly restless. Then someone heard on the radio that the world leaders' walkabout had been cancelled. The reason given was that it clashed with the execution of MacHeath.

The news spread quickly. The mood turned angry. People started demanding the money they'd been promised. With the world leaders off the scene, they turned on me instead. I was in real danger of being torn limb from limb.

If nothing else, I had learnt to think fast. I seized the one loud-hailer we'd found, and addressed the crowd:

'We're not going to be put off! We've come for the cameras, and we're going to find them!'

'Where are they?' someone yelled.

'At the execution!' I cried. 'That's where they are!'

'That's ten miles away!' came the reply.

'Then let's move!' I cried.

A few of us struck out for the nearest under-ground. Behind was confusion and dismay. But such was the desire for action, the movement spread. Just about everyone followed. We swept down into the tube and overwhelmed the ticket barriers. Today transport was free. We packed the trains so tight, the stink drove the fashion victims off at the next stop. People were wondering if there was a match on, and what kind of team could possibly have supporters like us.

No one was expecting us at Tyburn. It was like a carnival up there, till we arrived. There was a massive temporary enclosure, housing the giant video screen. Entrance was ten pounds. Speakers relayed the action from the death cell to an audience of ten thousand ghouls. Some were obviously drawn there by grim fascination. Others were lusting for blood. A few hundred fascists were chanting about law-and-order, protected by five ranks of police. The media were everywhere.

We had to get inside the enclosure. That was where the TV cameras were. I was thinking out our best approach, when I caught sight of a familiar face.

'Polly!'

Polly was near one of the entrances, with five microphones up her nose. I fought through to her.

'We're going to wreck this party,' I told her.

'Don't bother,' she said.

She looked a different person. No silk, no diamonds, no illusions.

'But it's a cover-up!' I cried.

Polly didn't seem to care. 'He wanted me to bribe him out,' she said. 'I told him I couldn't.' A wry smile came to her face. 'After all, we're talking about a lot of money. Not a post office book.'

The tannoy burst into life: 'MacHeath appears to be resigned to his fate. The doctor is preparing the syringe.'

An eerie silence fell as the doctor searched for a vein. Then . . .

'Let's go!' someone cried.

We went. We fought through the police lines and sent the fascists running like rabbits. We stormed the gates and swept into the enclosure. Before us was the giant screen, with MacHeath strapped in his chair, and the doctor hovering.

Next second it was blank. We'd pulled the plug. Fifty million homes would never know what happened to MacHeath. But they would know about us, the prisoners who mattered, the prisoners who fought back.

CARMEN

Adèle Geras

Based on the opera
CARMEN
Composer: Georges Bizet (1838–75)
Librettists: Henri Meilhac and Ludovic Halévy, after
Prosper Mérimée
First performed: Paris 1875

Ay de mí, querida, you are like all the others, all the foolish young women who come to me and ask me to tell them what lies in the future. What lovers, they want to know, what riches, what glory! And they never think, not for one moment of the horrors the cards may reveal. Because the cards never lie, *niña mía*, never. Their voices are soft, so soft that they are lost in the shuffling of the pack, so soft that they can disappear into the light of candles, into the shadows of the room. But I hear them clearly, because I am a true gitana, a true gypsy. And I see things too, because I watch and I move from place to place because it is in my blood to move, to travel as the red blood streams through the veins and into the darkness of the heart. And because I listen, and see and move from place to place, I can tell you stories. I notice how you lean forward to catch the tale, and I realize how eager you are, but I will tell you this: nothing in the story will change your mind. You will want me to look into my cards again, just for you. You will want your own future. You will not learn.

But listen: this place, this square has always been exactly like this. I have sat here for years, and very little changes. The soldiers in their guard-house over there, and the cigarette factory here. Who arranges such matters? Who decides to put lusty young men, far away from their homes and families so near to this . . . what should I call it . . . ? this beehive seething with young women, this place where the sweat drips between your breasts as you work, rolling the leaves, and where there's nothing to talk about but the handsome young men strolling up and down opposite, so deliciously dressed in their uniforms, shiny with gold braid and with pistols in their belts . . . ay, it's enough to make a young woman restless. They are a temptation. And the soldiers in their turn are tempted by the women. When the whistle blows and the women come out, every one of the soldiers stands to attention, if you understand me. I am an old woman and am allowed to be frank. You will understand me when you are older. All I am saying is, soldiers and young women . . . well, no one needs a pack of cards to see the troubles this arrangement may lead to,

Before I tell my story, you must know about Carmen. She was, in that beehive of a factory, the queen. She was a gypsy. She was a woman, and at the same time as wild and free as a tiger, or bird perhaps – a beautiful bird of prey. She was lovely to look at, of course, but so are many women. Carmen was worse than lovely: she was dangerous and irresistible, a dark pond into which one man after another plunged with no thoughts for his safety. Most managed to save themselves, but there was one who drowned, drowned in the waters of Carmen's eyes, one whose story you shall hear.

It began one day when a young peasant woman came looking for a soldier, her sweetheart from the days when he was still living in the same village. This young women was called Micaela, and was pretty in a soft and gentle way, like a small breeze blowing from the hills, like a deer, shy and docile. She had come, she said, with a letter from his mother for a soldier, a corporal called Don José. Morales, another soldier, told her that Don José would be arriving with the changing of the guard, and so she left, and said she would return. Perhaps she went to the inn for food. It was time for the midday meal, that much I remember, because the guard changes at noon or thereabouts, and the factory girls come out and sit under the trees in the square and rest for a short while from their labours. Carmen came with them, of course, and all the soldiers began to flirt with her, begging her to love them, to be theirs, and Carmen, being Carmen, laughed at them and told them what she used to tell them every day: that it was *she* who decided when to love a man, and when she did, he had better prepare himself for everything. We had all heard this before. Carmen was forever saying that no one would choose her, that love was like an untameable bird . . . we had heard it before. But on this day, Destiny that directs our lives arranged things so that Don José should hear her. Hear her and see her. No one noticed how he looked at Carmen, except me. He was like a rabbit, caught in the gaze of a wild creature, unable to move. I saw his eyes widen, his lips move, his breath quicken. Carmen saw it too. Such a smile crossed her lips, *querida*! She knew. This one was surely hers, and why not? He would pass the time.

As the whistle blew, calling the women back to their work, she walked close, close to where he was standing, and threw a rose she had had tucked behind her ear laughingly into his face. The rose fell on the dusty earth, and Don José picked it up. If he had left it there, then perhaps . . . but it is useless, useless to say 'if only'. These things are written down. Pre-ordained. By picking up the rose, Don José had decided. Carmen was like a sorceress, and she had cast her spell. Micaela arrived then, but it was too late. Oh, Don José was pleased to have a letter from his mother, and pleased to see his childhood sweetheart, and for a while they talked nostalgically about the old days in the country. Later on, when they kissed, I thought that perhaps there was still a chance. I heard what he said to her:

'You have saved me, Micaela, saved me from great danger.'

Micaela asked him what the danger was and he wouldn't tell her, but I knew. He sent messages and kisses to his mother with Micaela, who was going home the next day. After she had gone, though, I saw how he looked at the flower Carmen had thrown him, and I knew.

Then, all the peace of the siesta was shattered into a thousand fragments. A fight in the cigarette factory. Such things happened often, but in this case Carmen had wounded one of the, women. Zuniga, the Captain of Dragoons (and don't think he didn't have an eye for Carmen himself, because he did) decided that she must be placed under guard and taken to prison. And who was to be in charge of the guard? You have guessed, naturally. The threads woven by the Fates fall into such tidy patterns! They stood, the two of them, right beside me, there, and neither of them saw me, but I heard them. I heard them talking.

'You will let me escape,' Carmen said. 'You have to because you are in my power.' And she smiled.

'I don't know what you mean.' Don José blushed.

'You know very well. You have my flower, which is a magic flower that binds you to me. You are powerless. If you let me go, up there on that bridge, I will meet you at Lilla Pastia's tavern, and we will drink and dance . . . and I will love you because I have no lover and you have fallen into my path at just the right moment.'

I knew what would happen before Don José did. At first he was outraged at the suggestion, but gradually he melted. It was impossible for him not to melt before the fire of Carmen's voice, her body, her smell coming towards him in waves on the noon-day heat. She escaped. Up there on the bridge, just as they had arranged. Carmen fled. Zuniga had to blame someone, and so Don José was dragged off to some military gaol. Someone had to pay when the law was flouted, and besides, it probably suited Zuniga to have Don José out of the way.

Now I am a gypsy, and I travel. In those days, I travelled even further. Two months after Carmen's escape (and I hadn't thought about her for a long time) I went into Lilla Pastia's tavern, just outside the walls of Seville, and there she was. The place was full. Zuniga was there, a little drunk, with some of his dragoons, Frasquita and Mercedes were there, Carmen's friends from the factory, and naturally so was Carmen herself, shining like a candle.

The room was noisy, smoky, packed with people, most of whom, of course, I didn't know. Still, I recognized El Remendada and El Dancairo, two of the most famous smugglers in the district. Everyone knew them. The gypsy girls used to help them with their contraband, and Frasquita and Mercedes were boasting that it was their womanly talents for deception that had helped the men with their schemes. It was clear to me that they were planning something: wine or gold or tobacco, something was going to be taken over the mountain pass, and they were busy arranging it. I wasn't really interested. I was listening to a conversation between Zuniga and Carmen.

'Come with me,' said Zuniga. 'Your soldier has forgotten all about you after two months in gaol.'

'He will be free soon,' Carmen said. 'And I promised to wait for him.'

'He's free already,' Zuniga said. 'But where is he?'

Carmen smiled. 'He will come. If he is free, he will come.'

Just then, we all heard something outside, and someone, looking out of the tavern called:

'It's Escamillo! It's a torchlight procession bringing Escamillo into Seville!'

Probably you don't remember Escamillo, my child. No one is forgotten more quickly than yesterday's bullfighters. When Escamillo came into the bullring in his suit of lights, oh, the tight satin trousers, always satin, and the jacket heavy with silver embroidery, with the red cape over his arm, grown women fainted, and young girls threw fans and sweets and flowers down on to the bloody sand, and old women who had forgotten about such matters found their breath coming more quickly, and only some of them blamed it on the heat. Oh, Escamillo was beautiful, and he was brave with the bulls, *querida*, and his silver sword was sharp and quick and found its mark unerringly every time.

So on that night, everyone streamed out of the tavern and gathered round Escamillo and he told us something of the glories of the ancient dance of the bulls, something of the fear and the wonder and the thrill of marching into the ring Sunday after Sunday, facing danger, staring into the red eyes of Death. And of course, in all the throng, Escamillo's eyes fell on Carmen. He asked her her name, and she gave it to him.

'I will keep your name,' he said to her, 'as a talisman to guard me in the midst of danger.'

It was late when the bullfighter's procession moved off. Many people had gone to bed. Zuniga was drunker than he had been when I arrived. He was still pressing Carmen:

'He's free, Carmencita *mía*, and he has not come! Come with me, eh?'

On and on he went, and eventually wandered away. Meanwhile the smugglers were still planning and plotting at another table with Frasquita and Mercedes.

'Come with us, Carmen,' they said. 'Help us.'

And Carmen shook her head. 'I'm in love,' she said. 'I said I would meet him here and I am true to my word.'

'What if he doesn't come?' asked El Dancairo, but Don José arrived at just that moment, coming into Lilla Pastia's tavern with a white face, tired as though he had walked for miles. Carmen looked at him and her eyes like magnets drew him to her side.

'I would have languished even longer,' he said to her, 'in that stinking prison for your sake. I learned something there. With the flower you gave me, you claimed my soul, and now I'm yours.'

Then Carmen danced for him, and drew him close to her, and the music of the guitar throbbed between them, filtered into their blood.

At that moment, we heard a bugle sounding the retreat.

'I have to go,' Don José whispered.

'If you love me, you will stay,' Carmen was implacable.

'But then . . . I shall be a deserter.'

'We can run away,' Carmen whispered, 'over the mountain with the smugglers.'

'I cannot desert.'

'Then what kind of man are you?' she hissed at him. 'I want nothing to do with someone who hasn't the courage to love me. *Adiós*. Farewell for ever.'

Then Zuniga burst into the room and saw Don José.

'Come with me, Carmen,' he said. 'I'm asking you again. Why settle for a corporal when you can have a captain?'

You can imagine what happened next. Of course. When men and women and strong drink come together, what can there be but fights? In the end, El Dancairo and El Remendada and all the smugglers disarmed Zuniga and threw him out at pistol point. And all the while the time was passing, and still Don José was there. He had not left to go back to his regiment.

'Will you come with us?' Carmen asked him, brushing his ear with her sweet lips, running her fingers up and down his back, drawing him nearer and nearer to her fire. 'Will you follow us over the mountains?'

'I have to,' Don José answered, breathless with longing, and his voice broke with anguish. 'There is no other choice for me now.'

And he was right. I was watching, and I knew it. His path was marked, set out in front of him like a track cut into rock, from the moment he set eyes on Carmen, from the very second when he stooped to pick up her scarlet rose.

And so it happened that Don José and Carmen went up into the mountains with the smugglers. I went with them. I was young then and what else did I have to do? I followed and I listened. Nobody minded. I was a good cook.

The time passed and the cold came. Have you ever been up in those mountains, my child? How cold the wind blows there, and how hard the ground is for sleeping on! And life is difficult. Two things happened at the same time. Carmen began to grow bored with Don José, and Don José's guilt at his desertion from the army became harder and harder to bear. And as you know, one guilt comes always dragging another by the hand. He began to think of his mother, of his village, of sweet, pretty, good Micaela who loved him and whom he had treated so badly.

'Go!' Carmen would say to him. 'You are useless as a smuggler, which is a job for a real man. You are clearly only suited to play at soldiers, dressing up like a little boy and marching up and down. If you do not go, you will regret it.'

But Don José did not leave. He could not. Carmen still had him spellbound, enraptured. She had entered his bloodstream like a fever. He told her this and she shrugged her shoulders.

'You cannot fight your destiny,' she told him. 'One day, you will probably kill me.'

That night, near the camp-fire, Frasquita and Mercedes brought out the cards. They were laughing, wanting to seek out their lovers, hidden in the pack.

'I want a young and handsome one,' Frasquita said, 'who will carry me off for ever in his arms and love me into small pieces.'

'I want a very rich old man,' said Mercedes, 'who will let me go my own way and die quickly so that I am left a rich widow!'

Carmen came over to the fire. 'Let me take a card,' she said. She took one. The first card was a diamond, but the next was a spade and the one after that also. Two spades! Carmen knew what that meant, and so do I. Death, from whom no one can hide for ever, stared up at her from the pack.

'The cards do not lie,' said Carmen softly. 'They never lie. They speak the truth.' She left the camp-fire then, and stepped into the shadows, and the darkness swallowed her.

The next day, the smugglers left to cross the pass, and El Dancairo and El Remendada left Don José in charge of the supplies at the camp. I stayed too, wrapped in my blanket against the cold, and I saw her first: the young woman, Micaela. I thought to myself: she is braver than I gave her credit for. She has come to fight Carmen, and to try and win her man back from the temptations into which he has fallen . . . and no sooner had she arrived than she had to hide herself, because who should appear but Escamillo? Don José shot at him as he approached the camp, and even made a hole in his hat.

'Hey!' shouted Escamillo. 'Stop shooting! I'm looking for Carmen.'

'You took a risk,' Don José said, 'coming up here.'

'For a woman like Carmen, any risk is worth it.'

'What if Carmen is not interested in what you propose?'

'She will be, *amigo*.' Escamillo smiled at Don José. 'She ran away with some deserter, but that was months ago. No one lasts longer than six months with Carmen. She will be bored with the soldier by now. All the itches he produced in her at first, he'll have scratched over and over again . . . time for a change. She will be looking for something new.'

'Don't you know,' Don José said softly, 'how dangerous it is to take a gypsy's woman away from him?'

Escamillo then realized who was speaking to him.

'It's you . . . you're the soldier . . .'

I can tell you now, it was only the arrival of the smugglers and of Carmen herself that prevented Don José from killing Escamillo on that mountainside! I was watching and so was Micaela, as Carmen pulled Escamillo away and saved his life. El Dancairo stepped forward.

'You must leave this mountain,' he said. 'It is dangerous for you to stay here.'

'But I invite you all to the bullfight, to the corrida on Sunday, especially those who love me.' And he looked at Carmen. Everyone saw that look, flying through the air as though it were a physical object, a banderilla perhaps: one of those arrows covered in brightly-coloured ribbons such as bulls are stuck with to prepare them for the kill. And Escamillo's dart flew home. I saw Carmen smile, and run a moist tongue over her lips to cool them. She was ready for him.

Just as Escamillo left the camp, El Remendada

discovered Micaela, half-hidden behind the rock.

'Don't touch me!' she cried. 'I've come to speak to Don José. I have a message from his mother . . .'

'Micaela!' Don José rushed to her side. 'Oh, Micaela, why have you come here, all by yourself to this wild place?'

'I want to take you home,' Micaela answered. 'Your mother wants you back. Leave the mountain. Come home with me.'

'Yes,' said Carmen, mimicking Micaela's sweet tones. 'Leave the mountain and go with her. That's the best idea I've heard for a long time.'

'And leave you free to go to Escamillo!' Don José said. 'Don't think I didn't see the way you looked at him! I saw it. I know what the look means. You turned that gaze on me once.'

'Long ago . . .' said Carmen.

'But still,' Don José went on, 'you have burned yourself into me like a brand searing into the hide of a cow: forever. Only death can separate us now.'

'Do you not care,' said Micaela, 'that your own mother is near death? That is why she sent me . . . she wants to see you before she dies . . . to see you and forgive you.'

Then, something like a volcano began to erupt in Don José's bosom. A storm of feelings . . . all these words: storms, volcanoes and so forth I am using to convey to you the violence of his passion.

He was racked by love, by duty, by desire, by defeat, and by a dreadful jealousy that Carmen loved Escamillo now, and that her love for him had flown away, exactly as though it were the free, untameable bird that Carmen always said it was. This white bird of love had stopped for a while and let him hold it in the palm of his hand, and now it was gone, ready to alight on the shoulder of another man.

Carmen had lost interest in him. She was listening to Escamillo, singing as he went down the mountain. She made a small movement, as if to follow him and Don José prevented her. He grabbed her by the arm and turned his tortured gaze upon her.

'We will meet again,' said Don José. 'I promise you that we will meet again.'

'Break camp,' shouted El Dancairo. 'We're moving out.'

That was when we all left the mountain and came down into the town again, and that would have been a good time for the story to end: Don José going to see his mother and be forgiven, Carmen going to find a new love, and everyone, if not exactly happy, at least living in this world. But the cards, *querida*, the cards never lie and the cards said Death.

Some time later, I found myself in a shady spot outside the arena, just before the bullfight. I was selling carnations. Oh, I love the hour before the corrida starts! All the fine young men, all the ladies with their hair piled high under black lace veils and fixed with tortoiseshell combs, smelling so sweetly of perfumes . . . they bought my flowers, and laughed and opened their fans to make small breezes around their faces, and rustled their skirts like leaves all about them.

Then Escamillo arrived for the fight, with a crowd following him and Carmen on his arm. I had never seen her look more beautiful. No longer a cigarette girl or a smuggler's wench, she was a grand lady now: a queen for the king of the corrida, Escamillo himself. Her dress was crimson satin, frills and flounces from hip to ankle, and moulded over her fine bosom like glossy paint on a statue. I had never seen her looking at any other man as she looked that afternoon at Escamillo. It was clear to me that she loved him as she had never loved before. Frasquita and Mercedes came to whisper to her as they stood in front of me, buying red carnations. I heard what they said. Don José was here, somewhere in the crowd and looking for her. The Alcalde arrived then, and the crowd surged into the arena. Carmen waited. She was waiting for Don José. I had seen him, hiding behind a stone pillar. When everyone had gone, he stepped out.

'Frasquita and Mercedes said you were here,' Carmen said, coming towards him. 'They think you want to kill me.'

'I have come to plead with you,' he said. 'To

beg for your love, without which my life is nothing. Can you forget the past, Carmencita *mía*, and come with me to a new place where we can be together, start again?'

Carmen shook her head. 'No, Don José. All that is over. My mind is made up. You know I never change my mind, *hombre*.'

'But Carmen,' he pleaded. 'Do it to save us. I'll do anything, anything in return. I'll join the smugglers again. I'll do whatever in the world you want.'

'I can't,' said Carmen. 'Even though it may cost me my life, I have to be free . . . always free, whatever happens. Listen . . . do you hear them clapping in there? I have to go. I have to go and see.'

'It's Escamillo, isn't it? It's him. He is your lover now. Deny it if you dare.'

'Why should I deny it? I admit it freely and openly. Even in the face of Death I admit it. Nothing can change it. Now I'm going in . . .'

'No, no, stop!' Don José threw himself at Carmen, catching her round the knees, holding her back, preventing her from walking away. She looked at him with loathing.

'Kill me now,' she spat at him, 'or let me pass immediately.'

'Carmen, damn you to all eternity,' Don José shouted. 'Yield to me. Stay with me. Don't go!'

With one swift movement Carmen plucked

a gold ring from her finger and flung it to the ground.

'There,' she shrieked. 'Take it. It's the ring you gave me. I don't want it. I don't want anything of yours near me ever again . . .'

Don José lunged at her. At first I thought he was embracing her, but then her body slumped in his arms and he let her fall to the ground, his dagger still standing in her heart. The front of her crimson dress was stained a darker crimson, where the roses of Death were growing over her breasts, over her stomach and her thighs. Don José knelt beside her body. He had time to run away, but he didn't and the crowd coming out of the corrida found him.

'I have killed,' he kept saying, 'what I loved most in the whole world.'

Ay de mí, niña, the troubles in the world, the anguish and misery in the hearts of men and women that Love can bring! And still you want me to tell your fortune. Very well. Shuffle the pack, *querida*, and let us see how they fall, these cards that never lie, now, this minute, before you go back to your bench in the cigarette factory.

Records, tapes and/or CDs of the operas which inspired the stories in this collection are likely to be available to borrow from your local library. To help you choose from the many performances that have been recorded, the following are just some of those especially recommended in *The Penguin Guide to Compact Discs*. Details are given in the following order: title, composer, record company, main vocalists, chorus, orchestra, conductor.

MADAMA BUTTERFLY, Giacomo Puccini

Decca; Freni, Ludwig, Pavarotti, Kerns; Vienna State Opera Chorus; Vienna Philharmonic Orchestra; Karajan.

DER RING DES NIBELUNGEN:
DAS RHEINGOLD, Richard Wagner

Decca; Nilsson, Flagstad, Windgassen, Fischer-Dieskau, Hotter, London, Ludwig, Neidlinger, Frick, Svanholm, Stoltze, Böhme, Hoffgen, Sutherland, Crespin, King, Watson; Vienna Philharmonic Orchestra; Solti.

THE CUNNING LITTLE VIXEN,
Leoš Janáček

Decca; Popp, Randová, Jedlická; Vienna State Opera Chorus; Bratislava Children's Chorus; Vienna Philharmonic Orchestra; Mackerras.

DIDO AND AENEAS, Henry Purcell

Philips; Jessye Norman, McLaughlin, Kern, Allen, Power; English Chamber Orchestra and Chorus; Leppard.

THE MAKROPULOS AFFAIR, Leoš Janáček

Decca; Söderström, Dvorský, Zítek, Jedlická, Krejčík, Blachut; Vienna State Opera Chorus; Vienna Philharmonic Orchestra; Mackerras.

I PAGLIACI (THE STROLLING PLAYERS), Ruggiero Leoncavallo

Deutsche Grammophon; Carlyle, Bergonzi, Benelli, Taddei, Panerai; La Scala, Milan Chorus and Orchestra; Karajan.

CARMEN, Georges Bizet

Deutsche Grammophon; Baltsa, Carreras, Van Dam, Ricciarelli, Barbaux; Paris Opera Chorus, Schoenberg Boys' Chorus; Berlin Philharmonic Orchestra; Karajan.

THE BEGGAR'S OPERA, John Gay
(musical arrangement: Bonynge and Gamley)

Decca; Kanawa, Sutherland, Dean, Marks, Lansbury, Resnik, Rolfe Johnson; London Voices; National Philharmonic Orchestra; Bonynge.

J. F. S. LIBRARY

175 Camden Road NW1 9HD